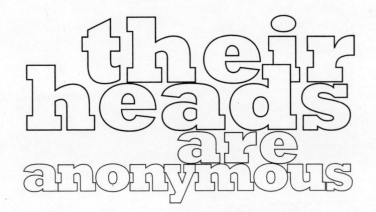

their heads
are
anonymous

Pulp Books
is an imprint of Pulp Faction
PO Box 12171, London N19 3HB
First published in Great Britain 1997
by Pulp Books
All rights reserved

An extract from this book
Palace of Nicotine appears in
Random Factor (Pulp Faction, 1997)

Their Heads Are Anonymous is a work of
fiction. Any character resemblance to
people living or dead is purely
coincidental

A CIP record for this book is available
from the British Library
ISBN 1901072029

their heads are anonymous

part one

in the
kingdom
of funfur

(one)
parry's
colossal head

The sunny blue European sky was there, and the cacophony of the ceaseless crowd, and the metallic sheen of the saucers as they hovered watchfully over the amusement park.

Parry blinked and tried to take a deep breath. The greasy homogenised smell of the Fast Foods Of The World Restaurant cluster was unaltered, and the sunburned hordes of visitors were still reckless for flavour-enhanced chow mein and wan doughy pizza, which some of them would bring up again later while riding on the Bullet Train or the Mach-3 Immersive. The insistent buzzing of the wasps remained clear as they darted hungrily around empty soft drink cups spewing from the mouths of overstuffed Marvin Monkey head disposal units. And far above it all the saucers didn't fly, but hung motionless in the summer thermals with oppressive clarity.

Parry was dressed as a rabbit on that hot afternoon. A rabbit with a name and a history: Gogo Bunny, one of the Bigger entertainment empire's roster of trademarked bringers of joy. Not in the same league as Maggie Gnu or Zero the Dog, to be sure, but popular as adorably anthropomorphisized mammals went. Self-obsolescent

3

lunch boxes, plastic tubes dispensing bland powdery sweets, stationery for teenage girls, polystyrene flavoured cereal; all these things and thousands of others bore images of the rabbit's big stupid head. Gogo was a nature spirit, a free-wheeling kind of guy in touch with his inner lagomorphic drives. Inside his fuzzy skin was a pissed off, overheated, sweating primate in his twenties whose job required him to wander through Bigger Amusement World dressed in thick grey funfur tat. Parry was determined to get through each day as best he could with minimum abrasion; the days he succeeded he went to bed if not a happy man, then at least a not unhappy one.

As he absently observed a group of South Asian Americans in their twenties eating clammy pre-filled lettuce and brie baguettes, he allowed himself to enjoy the strange kind of comfort which was sometimes to be found in the rank combination of cave and baked potato in a microwave that was Gogo Bunny's head. Ludicrous as it was the costume gave him a sense of identity through his very anonymity (I am not this stupid thing, I just wear his body, *it is not my fault*) and airless as it was it provided him with some breathing space. A space in which he didn't have to think. He liked that sometimes.

Parry headed away from the Fast Foods Of The World restaurant cluster, looking mostly at the ground so that he wouldn't have to see the saucers. No one else knows they're up there, he thought, then corrected himself: *thinks* they're up there. The heat. It's the heat. It's got to be. A subtle bob of the head to Marvin Monkey as they passed each other (don't you look stupid my hydrocephalic pal).

As he approached the Stalinist-lite Bigger International

Hotel, the trance of blankness invaded Parry's brain again as it often did while he was walking the Amusement World. Or when he was in supermarket aisles, waiting in queues, driving fast on the motorway, watching TV, making love.

Parry became more focused in the Family Plaza, where he found a disembodied head. It was a woolly cartoon pastiche of a gnu with its magnificent curving horns, sexy secondary sexual characteristic, reduced to useless foam appendages. Parry looked around in shock but there was no sign of the body that was supposed to be attached to the empty head.

The cardinal rule for all Bigger Amusement World cast was never to be seen out of costume. Ditto, especially ditto, the head. The Head. That was one of the absolute and non-negotiable commandments, that you were never seen dressed as one of the characters without your head. If you were, you didn't get the chance to exhibit yourself to the punters again because you were immediately outtahere.

If you needed reasons they were available, in writing and usually on a sheet of paper with bulletted lists:

★ Because you've broken the illusion that the characters are anything other than totally real.

★ Because you've destroyed the earthshaking moneymaking magic of the Amusement World.

★ Because you're obviously seriously *not* in harmony with the traditional nuclear family values empowering dreams can come true day/weekend/week/month (delete as applicable) of a lifetime total entertainment experience Amusement World type thang.

Then he spotted a girl in chocolate coloured lurex tights and a shaggy brown wildebeest body vomiting into the

Family Plaza's hi tech Orientalesque pool. Nobody except Parry seemed to notice. Even the man photographing his fluorescent pink brood by the fountain (I hope you realise you're inviting malignant melanoma, my friends) failed to heed the violently spewing half-gnu half-woman who must surely have appeared at the bottom left of the frame.

'Are you okay?'

(That has to be one of the stupidest things you've ever said in your life, Parry. Do okay people vomit?)

His chest tightened as the girl turned, weakly wiping the corners of her mouth on the back of one oversized white glove, and he saw who was wearing Maggie Gnu today.

Priscilla Kodak, unapproachably blonde, always smiling but piercing of gaze with it. Priscilla Kodak, whose liaison with Parry had seemed to him to owe more to tactical advantage than to his experience of normal human relations.

He noticed that the giant Koi had risen up from the depths of the pool where they habitually sheltered from the showers of tourists' pennies and were hungrily gobbling up the lumps in Priscilla's fresh hot puke.

At that moment she and the carp in the pool seemed separated at birth, with matching sets of bulging eyes and gawping gobs. Priscilla's overheated brain seemed incapable of processing what her eyes were seeing, vainly scrabbling around in the most neglected recesses of its memory for the most appropriate response to a seven foot rabbit enquiring after one's well-being. Instead of looking into the mesh covered mouth hole where Parry's voice came from, she stared deeply into Gogo's fixed synthetic eyes for a moment before her own became the eyes of a doll, wide and glassy, seeing nothing. She crumpled backwards slowly, like Sixties residential architecture dynamited at the foundations. She would have fallen in the water amidst the bloated fish had Parry not caught her awkwardly in his furry paws. The sign said Polite Notice Please Do Not Feed The Fish. Whatever.

With some difficulty Parry slung Maggie Gnu/Priscilla over one shoulder and plodded towards one of the many conveniently and discreetly located doors which led to the subterranean employees-only tunnels where they could escape, for a while, the thick heat which pressed down upon them both like a weighted tarpaulin.

No-one offered them any assistance. Nobody even seemed to be aware of a cartoon character carrying a semi-conscious girl dressed as a giant stylised South African antelope across the crowded Family Plaza.

When Parry thought to turn Gogo's eyes skyward, the flying saucers were gone. It was not the first time that Parry had seen them, and neither was it the first time he had wished never to see them again. They came and went at their convenience, not his, and he just didn't need that kind of bother.

Inside his huge head, the merciless heat of a midsummer afternoon continued to build.

(two)
priscilla dreams of giant eyes

Priscilla was one of the park's most popular ingenues, and she played both comedy and tragedy. At the moment she was in tragic mode, trying to explain herself as she twitchily combed out her starlet blonde hair. She was thinking on her feet—something she had never been good at—and trying to find one good reason why her supervisor should let her stay in the Amusement World's employ, instead of posting her underpaid overworked arse first class back to the real world with nobody to turn to and an unfavourable reference.

'I've got vomit,' she said, playing for time, 'in my hair. In my *hair*. Do you have any idea how that feels?'

Simultaneously, Talent Supervisor John was in the middle of an extended remix of the same tirade he'd been riffing on for about the past fifteen minutes with occasional interjections or clarifications from Priscilla, while Parry hovered silently nearby, just out of arm's reach like a timid squirrel at the park. Priscilla and the Talent Supervisor's conversations remained mutually exclusive.

Talent Supervisor John's three stars were worn with pride on a plastic bar above his name. He'd earned every tiny sparkling one over the course of his five year stretch.

His strategy for success within the Bigger organisation combined diligent mouthing of corporate person management marketing dogma with a willingness to put his face anywhere he'd put his hand and just enough spite to step on anyone that he needed to. Sometimes he would give them a good kicking on the way up as well, just to be on the safe side. He still had some way to go before he was a five star, and he liked to think of himself as humble in that respect.

'…And to cut a long story short, Ms. Kodak, you know the rules. In actual fact your agreement to abide by them is explicitly laid down in your talent handbook and implicitly accepted by you in as much as you have accepted a post here. Your contract is terminated as of this moment,' he said, unconsciously pawing at the badge on his fat little chest.

Priscilla stopped dead and did a 180 in the concrete corridor.

'Whoah, hold on there tiger. You're giving me the sack for not being able to work when it's like a hundred and thirty degrees in those heads? You are joking. Tell him, Parry.'

Parry looked at her for a second with his mouth open.

'It's hot,' he said, accidentally sounding unconvinced of a statement which he knew to be the truth. He shut his big mouth again.

Now the hand was fingering the fearsome looking crease in the grey Dacron but breathable slacks Talent Supervisor John was wearing.

'You removed the head.'

'I know. You can't sack me for that.'

'I just have. You've already been warned about other

behaviour which is not conducive to the kind of experience environment we're offering here.'

'But those were just warnings,' Priscilla said, genuinely uncomprehending.

'Last month you were recorded by securicams entering and leaving the park by, if memory serves me correctly, climbing the outer fence,' Talent Supervisor John said, obviously at the top of a list he'd been holding in memory for just such an occasion. Black mark number one against Priscilla's name.

'I was drunk,' Priscilla said, in an attempt at mitigation. Oops. Two.

'It was an electric fence,' said John. 'You could have been killed—'

'It wasn't switched on, though.'

'If it had been, you could have been killed. Which would not have been good for the public identity perception of the Amusement World. You've also been repeatedly warned against, and actually caught in the act of, shall we say entertaining men in the staff residences,' he said (tick), looking right at Parry, who was suddenly very interested in a red arrow with the word EXIT reversed out of it in white, '...which is for our female cast only, Ms. Kodak.'

'What can I say? I'm a woman, with a woman's needs, know what I mean?'

This was met with Talent Supervisor John's most slack, wholly unimpressed face of the day.

'You're sacked. You were sacked before we began this conversation, you were sacked while we were having this conversation and you remain sacked now that we've finished.'

With this he spun on one heel like one of the less convincing robots in the park above them and started to walk away.

'But,' Parry spat, almost involuntarily, Tourette's style.

Talent Supervisor John folded his short arms with limited success and raised his mono eyebrow.

'And?'

'But,' said Parry again, repeating his only conversational gambit until he could think of something else to say.

'Are we going to have a conversation consisting entirely of conjunctions, or do you have something of interest to say, Mr Parry?'

Parry blurted 'It's. Not. Her. Fault,' and immediately felt about as big as Talent Supervisor John looked, far away at the other end of the corridor. Under John's gaze he shrunk to the size of one of the lacklustre glove puppets at the shows which appeared in the Family Plaza at quarter to and quarter past and usually met with indifference at best, petulant lolly wielding toddlers at worst.

'Parry. While we're on the subject. Don't ever let me see you picking up talent in the park again. We have people in specially *scientifically* designed carts for picking up unconscious talent. You know that perfectly well. Just act in the capacity for which you are employed, if you like your employment here. Or even if you don't, to be brutally frank. Just don't make me look bad with your negativity.'

And he was gone.

Feeling that something was required of her under the circumstances, Priscilla yelled 'You piece of shit!' at the door which was swinging shut behind Talent Supervisor John, then she turned to Parry and sighed.

'I suppose the thing about woman's needs was a bit ill judged, wasn't it? Under the circumstances.'

'A little bit, yes,' said Parry.

She pushed her shoulder blades up against the white wall and slowly slid down it until she was on the floor with her legs stretched across the corridor and her head on her hand.

'Shit. What am I going to do now, Parry? I mean, am I fucked? Am I fucked or what?'

'I think you're probably fucked.'

'But I can't lose this job. I've got nowhere else to go. It's a shit job and I hate it, but what the hell else am I going to do? I've got to try and talk to John. Or something. There must be something.'

'He's not gonna change his mind. That's what he's known for. That's his thing. He never reverses a decision because that would make him look like some kind of human being instead of just another one of the robots. That would mean he'd made a mistake in the first place.' Parry rubbed his head absently with a huge rabbitty paw, 'I just don't know what to suggest.'

'Ah... Shit,' she said, extending one hand for Parry to help her up.

'Where are you going now?' he said. Holding onto her hand just a fraction of a moment too long, even though he couldn't really feel it through the glove.

'I suppose I'm gonna go and pack my bags and hit the fucking road, Parry,' she replied. But that's not the way it works, Parry thought. Not with you.

Priscilla shared a cramped room in the underground staff residences with a runaway girl called Marijne whose picture was on the wall of every police station between Zeebrugge and Groningen. Marijne told anyone who ever asked her about it that both her parents were dead, without ever specifying how they got that way. She was absent at the moment, so Parry sat on her bed and watched the packing machine that was Priscilla.

Marijne had colonised every horizontal surface in the bathroom with what looked to Parry like a fairly comprehensive selection of Europe's leading personal hygiene products along with some obscure ones which were, under normal circumstances, only available from your friendly local voodoo magic shop. After a few fruitless minutes of trying to sort out what was hers and what belonged to the Dutch hygiene freak, Priscilla swept roughly half of everything in the bathroom into a carrier bag.

'Have you ever—' Parry began.

'No.'

'You don't know what I'm going to say yet. I hate it when you do that. What I was going to say is, have you ever seen things when you've been wearing those costumes?'

'Like what? Like those little amoebas that swim around on your eyes when you look at the sun? It gets so hot in those outfits and you can't breathe and you're looking out through that little slit...'

Now she was stuffing clothes into another carrier bag. Luckily she had an unhealthy obsession with synthetic fibres, so most of her clothes were capable of being screwed up into ludicrously small parcels. With the kind of clothes she wore, Priscilla was sometimes the target of cruel jumble sale jokes from the other employees, but that was okay, she liked wearing cheap tack and possessed the total immunity to ridicule of a hyperactive toddler on tartrazine. Until now this had been an invaluable skill for her life inside the Amusement World.

'No. I mean like... hallucinations. Mirages. Mirages of things floating in the sky. Stuff like that.'

The bag was now so crammed that it looked like some kind of PVC sausage with Oxfam stuffing. With her hand still shoved inside it, she looked at him, trying to work out whether or not he was yanking her chain. Having decided that he was not, she told him that she never had and pulled her hand out of the bag. Now Parry was embarrassed, and all he could manage in response was a noncommittal to unconvincing 'Okay'.

She gazed at him, a carrier bag in each hand, looking like a fashion stylist's warped idea of a bag lady.

'It's funny you should say that, about things in the sky, though, because I've been having this dream for weeks. The same one every night, I think. Mixed up with others, normal dreams, but I keep having this dream about these giant eyes. They're floating over the park. Checking us all out. I can't remember very much else about it. So there you go. That was my dream. Come on. I've got to lock this door or Marijne'll think she's been robbed 'cause she's a paranoid bitch.'

She sighed as she turned the key in the lock.

'End of an era, Parry. End of an era.'

Parry walked beside her, his inflated fuzzy arm brushing against the cement wall, and studied her sadly.

'You're the last one, you know, Pris. Everyone I knew is

gone now. They've sacked everyone except me. I don't understand it. Most of them were like you. They never did anything to deserve getting the sack. Just stupid little things, here and there. And the new lot aren't the same. I don't even know any of their names. And there's something scary about some of them. Like they genuinely believe all the Bigger bullshit. It won't be the same. Priscilla. Hello. I'm talking to you.'

She was looking at a dozen limp bunches of lilies which had once graced the tables of the Bigger International Hotel and had now been dumped into a green plastic disposal cart which stood forlorn and unattended in the middle of the corridor.

'Isn't that sad?' she said. 'Isn't it a pity that things have to die?'

(three)
roach hotel

Ruthie Noon was a tangled mess of distant aches and little hurts as she walked carefully down the warm pavement of the Rue International. She had been hoovering up heavy duty painkillers ever since she left London, and now she rolled along on well oiled analgesic wheels with a slightly numb face and a dull but persistent sensation of pain in her breasts.

The operation had been an important one for her and she had waited for it a long time. During the unknowably long stretch of post-anaesthetic, hypnogogic time after Ruthie cranked open her eyelids one nanometer at a time to stare at a pristine white hospital ceiling but before she was able to exert enough control over the rest of her body to speak or move, she had decided that she had to get away from the grime and the grind of the city. As she lay on a firm comfortable bed feeling like a fallen shop dummy waiting to be clothed, she had vague recollections of people in white buzzing past her and of trying to tune out their voices as they talked beyond her line of sight; soft inanities about a holiday that one of them had either been on or was about to. Maybe this was what had given her the idea to go on holiday. For a few days afterwards she forgot about her promise to herself because her breasts felt like two WWII submarine mines, primed and ready to explode if they were jostled or prodded one more time.

But on the day she got out of hospital Ruthie calmly packed her bags with an all eventualities wardrobe and the requisite drugs, and got on a train. She didn't tell her doctor or her sister, or any of her several lovers, that she was going anywhere. She liked the idea of that, of just catching a train on the spur of the moment and riding it to wherever it went. So different from her holidays as a child: holidays that were meticulously planned by her father, starting as soon as they returned from the last one, holidays from a time when she had been called by a different name and had walked along the sea-front with her sister whose beautiful legs reminded Ruthie of slow motion footage of a deer, while the hair their father cut at home went stiff in the saline spray from the grey out of season sea.

Now it was summer and Ruthie was alone and she was walking through the automatic doors of the Bigger International Hotel of her own free will, past plush peach loveseats that nobody ever sat in and overbearing palms so healthy and lush they looked too real, as if they had OD'd on Baby Bio. She stopped for a moment and sent her gaze up through the vast sheets of gently sloping glass which made up most of the hotel's front. People entering the hotel invariably did this, just as unsupervised children inevitably tried to gob from the topmost galleries onto them. Like everything else in the Amusement World the hotel was oppressive and inhuman in scale. The view—upwards at a sky made unnaturally blue by a glazing process designed to prevent the whole place heating up like a brutalist greenhouse, or downwards from the top of the hotel to where hotel guests milled around randomly on the marble like bacilli under a microscope—certainly had the desired humbling effect. That's quite impressive, thought Ruthie, and I really do need a fag like *right* now and there bloody well better be a damn lift.

Ruthie had gone to sleep feeling travel fatigued and sticky from the heat, and she woke up after a few hours of drifting semi-sleep feeling much the same but groggy and with a dry throat to add to the list. She lay half on her face for a while with her eyes closed gently, listening to the comforting sound of the room and an intermittent furtive noise like somebody riffling the pages of a paperback.

She slowly opened her eyes and there was something on the pillow a centimetre away, a glorious widescreen cockroach monster eyes antennae legs too many legs brown shiny obscene carapace and she was up away and across the room before she had any conscious idea of what she was doing and she let out an involuntary, primal cry of disgust and fear at the thought of what it might have been doing to her or where it might have been crawling while she slept. Now that she was completely awake, she saw things like it on every surface in the room, horizontal or vertical, or whirring through the air on transparent papery wings. She hadn't known cockroaches could fly. There was something

21

disturbing about seeing them do that, exhibiting an ability that they normally kept to themselves. She had reflexively brushed the pillow roach, violator of her bed, across the floor where she watched it flick and curl for a few seconds before turning over onto its legs again and walking away. Her expensive room in the pristine hotel was full of insects. Her open case was infested with them, the complimentary fruit in the bowl had been tasted by the scavengers. One of them hummed past her face and she flapped it away. Some of the insects were walking in circles on the wall, turning brainless spirals on the eggshell finish paint, as if making some crude attempt to hypnotise her or themselves.

Ruthie took a deep breath and crossed the meandering flight paths of the cockroach horde to the door. She quickly slammed it shut behind her. A single roach escaped through the momentary gap and she watched it flicker away down the corridor and disappear into the stairwell. Ruthie knew she would be having words with the manager and that she would have some kind of recompense for her unpleasant afternoon napping experience, or there would be one V. pissed off and aggro woman in the lobby this afternoon.

Behind her in room 735, the insects cleaned and combed themselves aggressively in an attempt to remove carpet fluff, finger grease and other traces of contaminating human influence. They constantly conferred in infinitesimal squeaks and scrapings. After a while, they crawled back into the hidden angles and dim places from which they had emerged.

(four)
the ideal blank

His face looked a bit like what you would get if you used a black marker to put two dots of ink on your index finger's first knuckle, then waggled your thumb up and down underneath to make some kind of puppet. His name was Tom Doggo; he was unfeasibly tall, composed and inscrutable behind standard issue black shades.

He towered silently over the little knots of people who had just entered the park and stood in a mindless consumer choice trance, hypnotised by the incessant tumbling of the turnstiles and the blaring TV screens. Doggo was not like these people; he was not a tourist making the most of his nine days per annum holiday entitlement or a seeker after handshakes with oversized cartoon characters. His giant body, anchored on dinosaur bones, his lack of emotion, his almost total absence of sweat and his refusal to act a role made him the ideal blank onto whom any person he encountered in the park could project whatever they wanted, dismiss him as just another Amusement World artefact and then more or less forget they had ever seen him.

But he made sure that he saw and remembered them, because that was exactly what he got paid for. Doggo was a mystery tourist, retained by Bigger Amusement World's owners to test employees' patience with complaints of insects in the ice-cream, to goad them with rumours of children's arms yanked out at the socket by rides, to bug them with detailed enquiries about allergies and epilepsy. The responses he got, and the faces and voices which went along with them, were filed in his mind as adroitly and indelibly as Babylonian cuneiform on tablets. He observed a group of young men in V-neck teeshirts who might have been good looking if they had not been so wasted. How did they get cans of beer past the metal detectors at the gate, he wondered idly, without wasting too much processing power. He impartially assessed men and women and children with his Ribena dark eyes. Every day a thousand people bored him in a thousand different ways.

Doggo was a private investigator, and an extremely rigorous one under normal circumstances. When he had been self employed, he used to have something akin to fun as he sat in his office, watching the cars move along the street below his window or just sniffing markers all day if he wanted. He told himself it was no crime to be a repressed middle class man forced to take a job he didn't like or care about with an organisation whose values he despised; millions of people did it every day. Despite this reassurance, he couldn't help feeling ashamed at what he had come to: wearing a teeshirt with some arbitrary slogan (slightly too crisp at the collar) and shorts (slightly too tight), surrounded by people dressed as animals and dragged into some paranoid corporation's futile attempts at auto-espionage. Or perhaps MTI were just being prudent. The Amusement World didn't seem to be attracting as high a calibre of menial as once it had. Each influx of workers following the company's periodic employment purges seemed to exceed the last in surliness and plain lack of competence in Amusement World basics like sweeping rubbish or making themselves invisible to the untrained tourist's eye. He would have questioned the Amusement World's vetting of its new employees if he had cared in any way, shape or form, but if they didn't think he was good enough to run background checks it was their loss.

Decades ago as a child he had been coerced into playing the Virgin Mary in a school Nativity play, despite his already booming voice and big frame. He found himself experiencing a strikingly similar sensation now, asking of himself exactly the same questions as he had asked then: What am I doing here? How did I get from where I was, to here? Why do I look so stupid?

Then he spotted them. They pulled almost right up to the gates in a showroom clean pewter Volvo and climbed out. This in itself was unusual, given that the Amusement World's car parks stretched for kilometres in every direction. Usually only the shuttle buses drove people to the gates. The car crawled away, only to return twenty minutes later with another delivery of individuals from the same mould. People who didn't fit the demographic profile. People who looked like they had never been on a holiday in their lives but had maybe kind of heard that they existed and sometimes had to be endured by certain types of people. But for all this they had frighteningly even tans: their skin glowed orange and their demeanour radiated subtle menace and sinister intent. They were not at all fazed by the vomit inducing infotainment menu set out before them. They absolutely knew where they were going.

Paranoid, he thought, as an overpriced ice-cream in the shape of Gogo Bunny's head melted unheeded in his hand, not in his mouth. I'm being paranoid again. If I'm the mystery tourist and I'm employed by the corporation to report back on its own employees, who's reporting back on me? He imagined a Russian doll scenario, mystery tourists inside mystery tourists, big Tom Doggos outside little Tom Doggos inside big Tom Doggos. Spiral of paranoia. Metaparanoid.

At the same time he knew with utter certainty that they could not be ordinary punters. He was too good at this job not to notice that they were as utterly un with the Amusement World thing as he was. Mighty big blips on his pariah radar.

He accosted a passing dogsbody, who was making a desultory effort to sweep the omnipresent litter into a dustpan on the end of a long handle. Doggo asked the man if he knew anything about the people getting out of the Volvo by the gate.

The man narrowed porky eyes under the shadow of his baseball cap, and gave Doggo a look that said he would rather sweep him into the dustpan along with the crisp bags and lolly sticks than talk to him.

'I don't think I can help you with that, mister. I hope you have a nice day,' he said, and then took his brush and pan away with him without a second glance at Doggo. This was exactly the type of behaviour Doggo was employed to root out, but he let it lie for the moment.

He was more interested in keeping his eye on the Volvo men. Ten strides into the park, and they began to peel off in pre-arranged ones or twos like an aerial display team. Twenty, and they were a new virus floating blithely amongst white blood cells, seeking somewhere convenient and undisturbed to replicate. Thirty and they had been almost seamlessly swallowed up in the eddy currents of the unsuspecting crowd.

Doggo bent down and licked the melted novelty dairy product off the back of his hairy hand. It tasted like a Polo that had been stuck to the underneath of a sofa cushion for a year.

No children. Heavy aluminium luggage, unsuitable for a holiday. Why the hell would people like that be driving a Volvo?

(five)
bust monster

Charles Bigger was primally, congenitally horrible. He was born four years and one day after his famed grandfather's death in a golf cart accident on a course at the Amusement World. The fact that Charles had been born at all was a monstrosity. The potential for startling beauty had not expressed itself in his genes, and nor was he predisposed to turn people's heads or stomachs with his ugliness. But the coralline grey whorls of flesh behind Charles's ordinary face had distilled shocking poisons which eventually honed him into an unlovely monster. As he grew older his mouth turned in on itself to form a lizard lipped grimace, his eyes became holes cut in a Halloween ghost costume, his skin assumed the texture of a dried out flannel.

Charles liked to style himself a director of scientific and medical films, but the Biggers were one of those families whose lives were unfailingly drawn to the same hidden attractors of tragedy and misdeed generation after generation, and no amount of obfuscation could hide the fact that Charles was a pornographer of the vilest kind. Through a combination of default and inertia, he and transgression became lovers who stayed together because they knew neither of them would ever find anyone else to satisfy them like they did each other.

Charles's career progressed in grim parallel to that of his grandfather and namesake's life and work, the former a twisted replay of the latter. For both men, childhood was just a strip of film yanked through a projector and ruined in the process; a short, secret time of wounding to be endured. Later they began to hurt others instead of only being the passive recipients of pain and humiliation.

The first Charlie grew up inside his own head where he didn't have to look at his Aunt's acid scarred bomb site of a face, or experience the blows which came freely with her psychotic pastiche of maternity. Charles the younger's overwhelming memory of his parents was of the pair of them in single beds in the same room, which resembled a micro hospital ward. A gulf between them that neither could be bothered to cross. Wallowing in his'n'hers chronic invalidity.

Charlie's empire was built on a billion painted acetate cels, maniacal cartoon perma smiles, a sheltered world where nothing bad could not be faced and even the shadows were safely outlined in black. Charles carved a place for himself behind taped up windows, in unnamed continental warehouses, on the raw material of a conveyor belt of disposable teenage runaways and powerful zoom lenses. Both empires, the empire of flicker and the empire of flesh, seemed to create themselves as if possessed of an ambition which only used human lives as a convenient conduit. These dreams commodified colonised land eagerly, and they hungered for people's minds too. Empires need outposts, an army of sycophantic performing puppy cohorts eager to enact their will, slaves and consumers. Charlie and Charles both irresistibly drew such individuals to them, found them felt them fucked them chucked them and siphoned people's lives away from them bit by tiny bit.

As Charlie Bigger began to sense his own life ebbing away he fled to the Amusement World he had conjured from nothing. He cowered there like Hitler in his bunker, desperately trying to hang onto the wheel of the million ton truck without brakes that his entertainment empire had become. His lackeys tumbled out from the Amusement World; worker ants in search of chemicals and processes and Qabbalistic writings, anything which might eke out the hollow life of their king for a few years more.

Like his grandfather, everything was never enough for Charles Bigger. He could never be sated by simple depictions of men and women pretending to get it on. Rutting hard was what he wanted, foot long cow tongues and sides of beef, women, objects, forced into places they shouldn't go. Anatomic weapons. All of it captured on videotape for ever, infinitely replicable.

Corona had been violated in a million different ways before now by lovers, human and otherwise, whom she had stopped counting or attaching names to. Her life was measured out in girl/girl/boy or boy/boy/girl or girl/girl ad infinitum encounters on tape and off camera.

Her latest starring role was in Charles's newest production, the aptly titled BUST MONSTER!

Charles inspected filming from behind a row of monitors; in electron gun light he sat on a swivelling office chair, hunched and intense like a fetish in a museum cabinet.

Sometimes he gave them extra money on top of their fee,

a few quid if he thought they were worth it and could still stand under their own power after the film was finished. To the girls whose dads had crept into their rooms at night and made them keep secrets until they fled from that one abuser into a world which seemed to be entirely populated with them. To the chickens with hatred in their old eyes for the suits with wedding rings who bought them coffee in white polystyrene cups and made them bleed. Charles could spot them unerringly, the boys and the girls that nobody would pay attention to even (especially) if they got attacked, or simply disappeared and never returned. He picked them out and when he was finished, nine times out of every ten, he just dumped them back again and nobody was ever the wiser.

He loved nobody, not even himself. Charles's sick little dolls' world revolved around an axis of Temazepam, Mogadon, Nitrazepam, Dormonoct, Remnos, Rohypnol and Unisomnia.

As the camera pulled back to capture the image of her jerking head, Charles demanded that Corona look at the camera. She did, straight into the lens, one bruise forming on her bottom lip and another above her left eye. Corona was seventeen and she wasn't flattered by harsh white lights or cheap videotape. She had never been pretty and now her broken nose meant she probably never would be, either. She had not seen any of the films he had made, but she had heard things about Charles Bigger, things he was supposed to have done or had done to girls in his films, or to people who had obstructed his formidable desires out in the world. But it was also whispered that he was related to the founders of Bigger Entertainment and that he was rich because of it.

It appeared that those rumours at least were true, judging by the hangers on in his orbit. The expensive cars they drove. The odour of pollution that clung to Charles like cigarette smoke to clothes. The unbreakable silences he bought with his seemingly inexhaustible—and innumerable—bank accounts.

And she needed money. God, how she needed money. For drugs to kill the pain and for the man who called himself her agent, so he wouldn't make her go out on the streets like before, when an ex-soap-star once picked her up in his car and nearly killed her because that was his thing.

If she trod carefully, Corona thought, if she worked out just what it was she could give Charles that nobody else could, then she might have her first chance to claw her way out of the whole filthy scene. She was certain she could provide him with what he wanted, do whatever was needed and never have to do another film, never have to laugh and say how much she loved it through the agony, never be examined and patched up by a struck off doctor in a room with chipped, pea green walls ever again in her entire life.

BUST MONSTER! was supposed to be a one day shoot, nice and easy. She prayed in a secular kind of way that the Demerol would help her not to feel. About halfway through filming Charles got involved and events began to depart significantly from the script. In the course of the improvisations that followed she was grateful for the pills. They made her experience most of the things that were done to her in those hours as if she was looking at the tape of herself which was being made. At three the next morning Corona was black and blue, and red, and they left her lying in the rain down a culvert in an overgrown park that nobody went to anymore because they were too afraid.

Charles returned to his dank, empty house and washed his hands three times using first cold and then hot water. He washed the taps, his hands again, followed by the taps, three times. He followed this with a boiling shower that burned him pink, in the bathroom where he had committed his first rape.

To the uninformed eye, Charles lived alone in the crumbling house which represented the only portion of their haemorrhaging empire the Biggers had been able to hold onto. But to Charles it was full of ghosts, psychically imprinted upon its stained walls, scuffed floors and hideous furniture which had not been moved for decades, a museum of dementia.

Downstairs, to the left of the hall, was a room of uncertain original purpose in which his mother used to recline all day on a mechanical chair, looking out of the window at the trees because she was already practically a vegetable (even then) and had been for years, shuffling pathetically from one nervous breakdown to another. Sometimes, if she watched them long enough, she thought she could see the sycamores stir furtively of their own accord when there was no wind to move their spindly arms. The chair still faced out of the window, arched back and looking at the ceiling with its footrest extended, the only relaxed object in the whole building. The one thing that had changed since his mother had vacated the chair was that

Charles's video cassettes, the only babies he would ever have, had moved in and occupied one entire wall.

His parents' clinical bedroom that still smelled faintly of Dettox. The bed which Charles's father stopped bothering to get out of one morning, just laid there until the middle of the afternoon. As time went on he didn't stir until early evening. Finally he didn't even bother to get up to relieve himself, his level of pleasure in life reduced to tracking the passage of his own waste products from warm to cool as he lay in them.

The kitchen where the housekeeper found him eager for transgression and dealt out violence and sustenance, withheld blows for good behaviour and made him eat unspeakable things for bad. She was his love, his horror. Although she had been in her deserving grave for twenty years, thanks to her in Charles's house plates still rested exactly one inch from the edge of the stiff starched white tablecloth. Saucepan handles pointed at precisely forty five degrees relative to the front of the oven. Eating, using the stairs (left on the way up, right on the way down) or the lavatory, operating a light switch, were all to be conducted in flawless silence. Her power was perfect and absolute.

The study where he had received Messrs Dumont and Challenge, representatives of Millennium Therapeutics International, the ultimate owners of Bigger Entertainment and the Amusement World. The study's shelves were empty of everything except dust. The MTI mouthpieces wore cheap looking but undoubtedly very expensive suits and laughed in his face when he explained that he was willing to make them an offer for the park, to buy the place back or at least to put a Bigger on the board again. When they realised that he wasn't joking they were obliged to extricate themselves as quickly and politely as they could, explaining that he was welcome to buy shares through normal channels after consulting his financial advisor but *really* Mr Bigger buying it back it just doesn't work that way *really* and he decided then to have them both killed and see what their supercilious lying smiles looked like then.

The upper landing, where Charles came across his father hanged one day and experienced pride in him for the first and last time. He observed that the chair on which Donald Bigger had stood had been kicked away sideways at precisely ninety degrees and now lay parallel to the wall. The Gogo Bunny print tie he had used to throttle himself, so perpendicular. So pristine.

And the spartan room where every twenty four hours noisome dreams projected themselves on the insides of Charles's eyelids as he slept.

Tonight Charles dreams of echoing blank walls, soiled with age and crusted with chemicals leached out of the cement by thirty years of underground moisture. He approaches the familiar orange door. It slides weightlessly to one side beneath his dream hand. Beyond it is a concrete silo that harbours many darknesses. Caged lightbulbs recede into the dim distance and fluctuate randomly as if ready to wear out, but never do, no matter how many times he comes back here in his head.

In the centre of the otherwise empty room a gigantic stainless steel cylinder lies on its side. Its top has been peeled up and back from the inside, as if some giant sardines imprisoned inside have decided to make a break for it. Nitrogen boils into gas as it comes into contact with the foetid air of the silo.

His grandfather Charlie is here, plastic sheeting taped around his body, naked as only the dead can be.

Tears the freezer perished plastic from his face with nauseating old man sultana hands.

Wisps of the nitrogen he has been floating in are still evaporating from his tuft of white hair, escaping his open toothless mouth.

His skin hangs off of his chest like a second hand cardigan. Charles cannot tell if the limp, reaching hands are beckoning him or just grasping in mindless hunger.

He is there. He is there, under the Amusement World. Wanting something, wanting Charles. Wanting to happen.

Charles woke naked and sweating and pale on top of sheets that smelled of too many nightmares. He knew that people really do wake up in the night in a cold sweat sometimes, and he knew why. He ran his hand from his heart down across his white belly, checking the reality of himself, and wondered where his pyjamas had gone.

Eventually he was able to sleep again, lulled by incipient megalomania and an eerie understanding of Art Brut.

His was a universe parallel to our own, where Charles Manson was the fifth member of the Monkees and they had a top ten hit with their upbeat cover of Helter Skelter. Where women were bought and sold from catalogues, and could be returned for a full refund within twenty eight days if unsatisfied with the product, without affecting statutory rights. Where the difference between right and wrong was decided by whether or not he could get away with it. To him, crime was just an extra-legal variety of capitalism.

(six)
my life
as an electron

Parry's feet returned to their ceaseless journey around the Amusement World's superheated thoroughfares. Priscilla slipped away into the crowds, saying that if Talent Supervisor John wanted her out then security would have to find her first. She meant it, too, and both of them knew that if Priscilla was determined to lose herself in the park then John would be forced to use a pack of slavering hounds to track her down.

Soon after Parry had arrived to work at the Amusement World, he'd taken one of the pastel electric carts he had seen puttering around the park on various errands and gone on an exploratory tour of the place. He got himself so comprehensively lost that his vehicle—the jumped up golf cart—ran out of power, so he left it where it conked out for some maintenance guy to find and tried to find his way back to where he had started from by following the allegedly helpful signs. Eventually he grasped the essential futility of this approach; all the signs (Ella Fun says: FOLLOW ME FOR FUN!) were there merely as scenery, and pointed so arbitrarily at their destinations as to be useless.

Now he just let his feet pound the pavement,

disconnected from his brain, and surrendered to the rolling rhythm of heel and toe hitting tarmac. I could die in here, he thought, and the costume would just keep walking and walking and walking and nobody would ever realise that I was dead inside here.

Then Parry was waist deep in tiny children.

'Gogo! Gogo!' they squawked, yanking on his hands like if they did it hard enough, badly sampled sound bites would come out of his mouth.

Parry did his best HI KIDS NICE TO SEE YA wave along with the jaunty bob of the rabbit's oversized head which he'd had to master before graduating from Talent Induction. That was four years ago, and he still had no stars, a cause for considerable shame in the eyes of career yes men like Talent Supervisor John.

One particularly revolting specimen of childhood, a negative role model for the under fives with coconut hair and chocolate all around his ugly little gob, beckoned Parry downwards with a floppy wristed gesture. Assuming that the wee one wanted to embrace his fuzzy alter ego and plant a naive sticky kiss on the rabbit thing's furry face, Parry complied. The mouth, the mouth. Worse in closeup.

'You're not real,' it said. 'You're not. You're just a man in a suit.'

Blasphemy. To compound his sin, Coconut Head then proceeded to peer through Gogo Bunny's mouth at the perpetrator of this innocence shattering deception.

Parry had learned how to deal with this kind of challenge to the Amusement World's authority at Talent Induction. Firm, decisive action was obviously called for. But the only thing he could think of in his distracted, sweating state was to persist with the HI KIDS NICE TO SEE YA and hope that the kid would give it up. He couldn't recall much else from his talent induction because he had been more interested in the desperate graffiti carved into the table in front of him than in droning lectures on the finer points of finding your inner bunny. How difficult could it be, for Christ's sake?

'Listen. Listen to me. You're not real.'

Coconut Head turned to the little dark haired girl at his side for corroboration, but she was exhibiting response 3 (Three) to grown men and women going around dressed in the style of cartoon personalities. About three years old, she stared up at Parry agog, oscillating rapidly between bewilderment and abject horror. Coconut Head himself was exhibiting the second response in the Bigger schema; rejection of the Amusement World Fantasy Experience. Response the first, and the one most heartily endorsed by the corporation, was the kind of mindless adoration—also known as THE SWARM—which Parry was experiencing now from the other children milling around his feet with gentle prodding from nearby parents (not necessarily their own). He felt slightly light headed from the still rising heat. He could almost see a glass of cool water floating, cartoon style, before his eyes.

Parry bent down close to Coconut Head's face, close enough to be heard by him and him alone.

'You listen to me,' he said through the rabbit's mouth. 'Just piss off back to your mum and dad and don't give me any shit, alright?'

Coconut Head gawped.

'What?' Drawn out, rising at the end, the child

somehow managed to make the word multisyllabic.

Parry felt the bile rising in his throat, tasted it burning on the very back of his tongue.

'Out of my way,' he said. 'Out of my way. I think I'm going to throw up.'

Parry couldn't help himself. Parry was sick inside his head.

He burst through the children, spume on a sea of families, and began to lope away, hindered by his gigantic feet. The glass of water which had hovered before him had now been replaced by the words AUTOMATIC DISMISSAL as he ran, almost blind with panic, through the park. His puke also floated distressingly close in front of him. He was afraid of dying by choking on his own vomit and revolted because he couldn't keep away from it. If he'd had anything else to bring up he would have done, and then he would surely have drowned in the hot rising tide of throw up. Thinking this made him feel even worse but he couldn't help it because he was already caught up in the delirious circular logic. The vile hot taste of it. The lumpy feel of it on his chin.

His stomach was having violent convulsions, his skin in the dark of Gogo's head was clammy and grey. His vision was blurred, his view reduced to a mad letterbox format collage of bovine tourist faces and helium balloons, blaring widescreen acid colour cartoon loops superimposed with flashing computer generated reminders about under-subscribed rides, burger stands and interrupted queues.

One is never seen without one's head, ever. Automatic dismissal. The sound of the blood in his ears rushing became a constant intrusive buzz, like a Dust Buster had been switched on inside Gogo Bunny's head.

Parry wondered how he'd got onto the tracks of one of the rides, but it was more pressing at that moment to work out how to get off again. He wasn't even sure which ride it was until he saw the insane grinning face of Marvin Monkey moving towards him along the rails in adrenaline slo-mo. Marvin's Barrel of Monkeys Bullet Train took its passengers on a warp speed drive-by of a robotic Marvin and sundry primate themed animatronic cohorts frolicking in an idealised tropical setting. On its way it took thrilling plunges into rubber piranha infested waters and through impressive looking stay dry waterfalls. Parry could hear screaming, although he wasn't sure whether it was because someone had spotted him in the Bullet Train's path or if it was just because the ride was going so breathtakingly fast.

And the buzzing in his ears. One is never seen without one's head, ever. Automatic dismissal. One is never seen and (contact will be re-established after a fire). The Bullet Train was coming towards him too fast, Marvin's maniacal smirk zooming in to fill his vision. Parry couldn't move. A huge buzzing, too big for his ears to contain, phasing in and out of coherent speech like a badly tuned in radio (contact will be re-established after a fire contact will be re-established after a fire contact will be re-established...)

He stagger-fell over to one side and maybe he was just clipped by the Bullet Train as it rushed on without caring or noticing but then he was falling with voices droning in his ears and thinking nothing, falling into a service shaft and he didn't care how deep it was because it was better than being splattered on Marvin's fibreglass face like a motorway insect in the summer and (contact will be re-established after a fire...)

Parry landed hard on his left shoulder or it could have been his right because it was hardly relevant under the circumstances and lay there, stunned and numbed, underneath a slowly dripping pipe. Ha ha, he thought, I'm dying for a drink I'm dying. It was dark there, and cool too, and he was zipped up in the droning OM sound of distant subterranean machinery and the blood so loud in his ears. Parry continued to shrink until he became an electron, so small that he had no position in time or space. He became a wave of probability. Anything could happen to him now.

(seven)
a whim of steel

Talent Supervisor John's hands worked circles on Priscilla's shoulders in the darkness behind the façade of the Enchanted Chateau. Keeping her job had been Priscilla's idea, oral sex had predictably been his. Far from discussing the renewal of her contract, all she had achieved so far was dusty knees, a crick in the neck and an aching jaw. Behind John a large sign bearing the words CLOSED FOR ERECTION OF NEW EXHIBITION was propped on its end, so that from Priscilla's viewpoint the word ERECTION appeared to emerge from the top of John's head. Every time she noticed this it made her want to crack up, but she decided that giggling with John's dick in her face probably wouldn't be taken with the kind of good humour which was conducive to getting back on his good side. She was bored, her attention wandered, John thrust himself forward and Priscilla gagged.

'Christ!' she said. 'What are you trying to do, fuck my lungs?'

'Do you want your job back or not? I'd be bending the rules, but I'm prepared to do it, you know. If I think it's worth the trouble.'

She wrinkled her nose. 'Goodness me, thank you, your highness.'

He looked ridiculous with his dick sticking out of his perma creased slacks like the last cocktail sausage at the buffet, and she told him so. He told her to stop complaining and finish what she had started. To show a bit of commitment for once in her career. She got off her knees so she could look him in the face instead of the groin, although the former was only marginally more appealing than the latter.

'Oh… just put it away.'

Quite deliberately she turned her back on him and walked away.

'Priscilla, we haven't finished yet. If you want anything from me, you have to do your part of it to my satisfaction.'

She heard the sound of John's zip moving up and down and felt his hand on her shoulder, felt him nudge up against her like a perverted bumper car and speak into her ear:

'Just finish it with your hands. It'll only take a minute.'

'I'm sure it will. Do it yourself. I'm sure you've had enough practice. How can I make it any clearer? It's not worth the bother. You can keep your crappy job.'

'Indicating either that you suddenly have scruples or that you just don't like getting your hands dirty,' said John with a snort, rearranging his penis in his ugly trousers.

'Do fuck off. I'm not the Amusement World's resident call girl.'

The hand slithered down to handle her right breast.

'That's not what I saw written in the gents' toilets.'

Priscilla removed the offending extremity and turned to John, surprising him as much as herself by grabbing a fistful of his shirt and holding his three star name badge tight in her white knuckled hand.

'John. Just please peel yourself away from my existence, alright? I'm gone, okay? I'm gone.'

Then he had jump cut hold of her wrist and was pulling her back into the abandoned tower of the Enchanted Chateau which was currently being used for the storage of pieces of wood and old signs and for attempted rapes and constituted a considerable fire hazard, and he was trying in vain to get his clothes off and hers at the same time, and before she knew it she had a spanner in her hand.

It made a surprising and satisfying cracking sound as it came into forceful contact with the left parietal of John's skull.

Priscilla's expectations of the effects of blows to the head were primarily influenced by Agatha Christie films and playing Cluedo, so she was unsure whether she had really meant to kill him (Priscilla Kodak in the Enchanted Chateau with the Spanner) but she certainly would have been pleased to concuss the motherfucker and give him a good lump on the head to remember her by. Instead of knocking him cold, all it did was make him angry and her scared at what he might do next. He did up his slacks and began to furiously sort through his bunch of keys and smartcards. He started backing away from her, one bloody hand clasped behind his ear and the other pointing the key to the tower at her like it would keep her at bay.

That was how Priscilla came to be locked in the dirty tower of the Enchanted Chateau like the cut price princess that she was. She could hear Talent Supervisor John behind the door as the lock clicked home and sealed her fate.

'You mad bloody bitch. I don't believe you'd do a thing like that. I'm going to get security and have them throw you out and kick your arse if you so much as say a word. Not one word. Ow. *Ow*. Christ…'

'Talking to yourself, John,' she called. 'First sign of madness.'

Knowing the cliché would annoy because it was the kind of smug idiocy that he would use himself.

'Bloody bitch,' he said, half to her and half to himself. 'Bloody bloody bitch.'

Priscilla looked up at the tower which rose dark and dusty above her, hollow and fake like everything else to be seen, felt or tasted within the park's borders. She watched the specks of dust that were floating in the light from narrow Gothic windows near the roof and wondered if there was any way she could possibly climb out before John came back with reinforcements.

(eight)
palace of
nicotine

Doggo drifted aimlessly into a bar, picked up a girl and she took him back to her hotel room where they talked a bit and then made love without a word. But all this took place inside the Bigger Amusement World where nothing could ever be that simple.

The Olde Englishe Pub (luckily somebody had seen some sense and thought better of a third extraneous letter E) had a bar and so, technically speaking, was a bar. Its drinks were served in authentic tankards—unknown in any real pub at any point in history—by buxom within the boundaries of a family environment English serving wenches who were mostly French. It had a low beamed ceiling, but not so low as to lead to concussion followed swiftly by civil action, unless you were unusually tall. The top of Doggo's head brushed the beams when he stood. The antique books and rustic hurricane lamps were superglued to the shelves and the dart board had never been used because there were no darts. The place was full of haggard fathers in hiding, drained by days or weeks of unrelenting and unwanted time with their normally decorative wives and children. What the Olde Englishe Pub did not have was alcoholic drinks. Or ashtrays. The kind of no ashtrays which means there are no ashtrays for a reason and the reason is because you are not under any circumstances going to smoke in here pal.

Doggo sat on a bar stool for an indeterminate length of time with his head tilted towards the ceiling, not even sure of what he was looking at or what he expected to see up there.

'It's far too clean, isn't it? That's the problem with this whole place.'

Doggo turned his head, taking her in with one swift imperceptible scan. Strong legs, long legs in 501s, almost too tightly belted like a kind of denim corset. White teeshirt. No attempt to hide the fact that her breasts were very much there and worth looking at, but not screaming out get a load of my knockers either. Tired hair fell without enthusiasm around a face that wasn't contemporary feminine. The kind of face normally described as striking; the kind of face that nobody would necessarily pick but would be quite pleased to have if that was the way things turned out.

'I'm sorry?' said Doggo.

'I noticed you'd been looking at the ceiling for a while, and I kind of wondered what you might be looking at,' she said, starting to put her hands in her pockets but then thinking better of it and placing them gently between the beer mats on the bar instead.

'Then I realised what it was. It's the wrong colour. It's too clean. It's like practically everything here. Everything's too clean. Pub ceilings should be… amber.'

Doggo nodded.

'You've been watching me.'

There was no accusation in his voice, just a statement of

fact. Strange for him to be noticed at all, let alone to be watched with such obvious interest. She looked at him with a slight smile deciding whether or not to show itself fully on her lips.

Making dotted lines with his eyes, he indicated the Silk Cuts peeping out of her right hand jeans pocket.

'I'm dying for a fag.'

She leaned forward slightly, almost resting her chin on an elegant hand. And smiled.

'I knew you would be. Come back with me to my palace of nicotine and you might be in luck,' she said.

Ruthie sat on the edge of the bath in the en suite of her new fluorescent lit hotel room. Fluorescent strips are not designed to flatter anything except meat and electronic appliances, yet Doggo revised his estimate of her upwards. Ruthie, wearing only lipstick, was strikingly beautiful.

Deliberate in her actions, Ruthie slowly pulled the pack from her pocket and placed it down on the cistern lid beside her. She searched for her lighter in her other pocket and found it. She picked up the cigarettes, almost in slow motion, drew one out and lit the tip gently, taking a short drag with a slight nose exhale. She put the lighter down on top of the pack. Then, finally, she took the first full drag, holding it in and then exhaling a perfect cone of downward smoke.

'I bet there's some things you'd like to ask me,' she said.

Doggo had been transfixed. He shook his head slowly.

'I don't have a clue what I'm supposed to be asking you. It's just…'

They had gone together to Ruthie's hotel room, to the frank but inexplicable displeasure of the man at the front desk, the Bigger International's self-appointed arbiter of morality. (In the mystery customer department of Doggo's brain, a black mark was registered). They had told each other their names and ritually exchanged mutterings of I'm not in the habit of doing this. Doggo found a strange growth in Ruthie's jeans.

'… It's just outside my area of expertise, that's all.'

Ruthie was a transsexual. Very clearly in the trans stage of being sexual.

'Show me,' Doggo said and Ruthie did, pulling her teeshirt up over her head and slipping out of her bra to show the still soft, pink scars of the augmentation mammoplasty. The feeling produced in him by the sight of her altered and scarred, very beautiful body was far beyond anything of its kind that Doggo had ever felt before. It was memory and recognition, only barely remembered and half imagined. Like something in a dream. The sort of dream that comes back to you at random, unexpected moments making you wish you could dream it again and return to the place in your mind where it has been living secretly all the time.

She didn't want to look him in the face, so she inspected the inoffensive royal blue Flotex carpet, as if the answers to unspoken questions could be found written there in scuff marks and vacuum cleaner stripes.

'I suppose it wasn't a very nice thing to do,' she murmured, 'not to tell you before. Before you found out for yourself. I feel bad about it.'

'But the world's full of people who do things that aren't very nice,' he said, taking her girl slender wrist in one broad hand.

Ruthie looked into Doggo's face as he leaned against the sink, then over his shoulder at herself in the mirror.

'Or have things done to them that aren't nice either. So what?'

Ruthie looked deeper into his hard face with a strange unreadable expression on her own.

'I'm just so used to being greeted like I was some kind of terrible monster. Some kind of scum. I suppose that's why I ended up here, of all the places I could have gone to,' she said, turning over Doggo's hand and comparing the tininess of her own in wonder. 'Just to be amongst the cartoons. Because I feel like one myself.'

'I bet you make some people who were born women sick that they don't look like you.'

'And some people think that what I've done—' looking down at herself, her creation, '—is sick. Against nature.'

'Of course it's against nature,' Doggo said, studying Ruthie's face closely for seams or flaws and finding none. 'So is Maggie Gnu.'

'What do I do now?' she said. 'What do we do now?'

'Tell me,' whispered Doggo, and Ruthie did, perched on the edge of the bath.

'I'm having my body surgically altered to become more beautiful and more feminine,' she said. 'I know I'm capitulating to a particular set of norms imposed by the white Anglo-Saxon media, but it's just something that I feel like I have to do.

'It's because I think that the body finally can't be touched by all our cynicism and shifting systems of belief that we no longer have any faith in anyway,' she said. 'My own body is the only place where there's any basis for real values or real change.

'I remember laying awake at night with the memory of a boy's skin on the tips of my fingers,' she said. 'Something innocent, laying there thinking of some innocent forbidden place like the curve of his shoulder or the grooved skin where the elastic of his pants cut into his waist.

'I want to mould myself,' she said. 'Shape myself into something that was never here before. I want to be myself, I want to be myself now and for the rest of my natural life which ergo means forever.

'Some of the men I've slept with,' she said, 'have been effeminate beyond the most desperate dreams of any woman. Some of the men I've slept with didn't even know that the Village People were gay.'

Doggo noticed that there wasn't enough air in the room, something not powerful enough about the air conditioning. He kissed Ruthie's mouth, which tasted like coffee and cigarette breath, slightly sour. Gently drew his fingers along the semicircular cicatrices which ran beneath her new breasts.

'Let's turn the television off,' he said, leading her by the hand out of the bathroom.

Ruthie looked at the blank, inert screen and then at him.

He shrugged. 'I thought... I could hear voices. I thought that the telly was on when we came in. I thought I could hear it. A news report, like a news flash or something.'

'Could've been in the next room,' she said, pointing out

the cord which lay limp and unplugged against the wall. 'I didn't hear anything.'

Doggo sat slightly hunched on the edge of the bed with his meat hands hanging between his knees.

'It doesn't matter,' he said. 'Come here. It doesn't matter. There's so much of it that you hear it even when it's not there. It's like you don't need an aerial any more to pick up TV transmissions. And I think telly is responsible for everything that's bland, boring and completely fucked in the world.'

She sat beside him, thigh to thigh.

'Are you a reader, then?'

'No. No. I don't read any books,' Doggo replied, looking genuinely surprised to hear the words coming out of his mouth. 'I don't think I ever even touch them or hold them, now that I think about it. It's like they're alien objects. Like I'm afraid of them. Afraid of receiving information because I might not like it, or I might not like what I feel I have to do because I know a certain thing. In my life, I mean, not in my job. Because my job is information—'

Ruthie took hold of his hands again. Fascinated by his hands.

'One thing,' she said quietly. 'I'm not a woman trapped in a man's body. I'm a man with tits. Or a woman with a dick.'

Doggo looked thoughtful for a moment, his eyes almost lost in his face, heliograph signals in flesh valley.

'That's cool,' he said.

The cockroach sitting on Ruthie's suitcase interrupted the Sisyphean task of cleaning itself to watch them while they kissed hard and time stood still as they made love. Tactfully, the roach kept to itself any opinions it might have had about the pointless eroticism which took up so much of a mammalian life.

(nine)
hand of glory

He checked his expensively heavy watch and swung smoothly out of the flow of the crowd. In his early thirties, eastern European looking except for his good haircut and deep, factory perfect tan. His aluminium briefcase was small and new. His dark glasses were very dark. His short sleeved shirt had been fashionable maybe ten years ago. His denim shorts were so clinically done that they looked amputated rather than cut off. In a tunnel which sloped gently downwards behind a mesh gate, all of the clothes went but the dark glasses stayed. He was shrugging himself into a one size fits nobody Amusement World Security shirt when somebody got in his light.

'Are you security?'

A dumpy troll of a man, who gave the impression of being almost as broad as he was tall, stood looking through the mesh with one hand to the back of his head. Blood seemed to be coming from somewhere behind his ear. Security squinted through smoked glass eyes and read a name, John, above something illegible and three gold stars. He shook his head.

'I need security. Look,' he said, extending three red

fingers. 'She's bloody deranged. I told her to leave and she wouldn't go.'

Security studied him like a frog pinned to a board, awaiting dissection.

Talent Supervisor John was not used to such disrespect by omission. He had three stars, and three stars meant that security owed him a certain amount of obedience in the feudal scheme of the Amusement World. He opened the gate and approached Security.

'Listen, am I making myself clear?' he said. 'An employee, ex-employee actually, attacked me. Hit me with a bloody spanner. Don't just stand there.'

The man pulled up his shirt slightly as if he was fishing for change in his pocket and there was a startling pop which echoed down the corridor. A neat hole was made through John's polyester shirt just below his three stars, and another slightly larger one as the bullet shattered his scapula, left his body and took a chip out of the wall behind. John's heart stuttered to a halt and he died.

Security looked at his wrist again. He hadn't wanted to do something risky like that, not now. Not when they'd be starting soon. After that they'd be able to do exactly what they liked.

They were visible here and there, stationary buoys in an ocean of bobbing heads. All over the park, hard looking men with hard faces stood still and looked hard at the internal AmusemenTV monitors, giving the endless loops of cartoons and promos more attention than they would appear to warrant unless one was a member of a Christian group dedicated to finding the non-existent obscenities and attacks on traditional family structure in children's cartoons, or a die hard deconstructionist.

At the moment Marvin Monkey is being induced, against his will, to take a shower. To protect himself from further indignity, he produces a full pre-Scuba diver's suit with a metal helmet and puts it on. There it was. Cartoon hand, palm forward, five fingers.

Five.

After a blow to the head, Gogo Bunny dances through a field of sunflowers dressed as a girl, under a blue sky. Little birds are fluttering about as if they are drugged. Then against a black background, an ideographic hand, an abstract hand.

Four.

An ultrabrite smiling nuclear family are ushered into the vast pastel lobby of the Bigger International Hotel in their father's patriarchal arms, following a strip of perfect vermilion carpet which is not there in reality. The family unit is welcomed by a coiffured and beaming array of bellpeople and receptionists and chefs and chamberpersons. A laughing young uniformed woman spreads her hands towards us/the family and sprinkles us with magic. Mum and Dad keep on moving through the lobby but up as well into the crystalline atrium in a swirl of golden dust and somehow their clothes are gone and they're looping the loop and they're wearing their swimming costumes and relaxing in the turquoise pool, reading magazines as they drift carelessly with their arses stuck through the centres of inflatable doughnuts. Mum and Dad flicker blip stutter and the hand is there.

Three.

Son and daughter plunge up and down on the Bullet Train, fill their arms and their bellies with food representing all the major food groups (Saccharine, Sticky, Bland and Salty) from the Fast Foods Of The World Restaurant cluster, are gathered up in Ella Fun's arms and they're laughing with joy as she points with her trunk and shows them the whole vast Amusement World spread out before them, for them. There's the hand, Peace Sign or Up Yours, it's hard to tell.

Two.

An old man with swept back white hair, film processing from the Sixties which makes all the colours look edible, even on people. I'm Charlie Bigger and this is my World. He rises from his chair and sits on the desk. Jump cut and he's back behind the desk. He rises and sits. I'm Charlie Bigger and this is. Jump cut. He rises. I'm Charlie. Drums beat double time. I'm Charlie. My my my my my my. World.

One.

An army of children waves and beckons. Some of them do crappy, uncoordinated versions of contemporary dances. They come in a commercially prudent variety of shapes, sizes and colours. Amusement World logo, bland arpeggio.

Zero.

End transmission. Normal service will probably never be resumed.

The sign above the gigantic main entrance gates said Welcome to Bigger Amusement World. It was flanked on either side by Marvin Monkey and Zero the Dog in gigantic fibreglass effigy. Entry was generally "not recommended" after a certain time in the afternoon and so in practice forbidden, so even if anybody had been paying attention they would not have thought it particularly strange when the great steel shutters slid down and clunked decisively into place. The standby lights on the alphanumeric pads next to the emergency exits and staff entrances blinked out all over the park, disabling alarms and locking most of the doors shut. A few employees got locked inside staff toilets or shower rooms, but nobody could hear them calling out and so there they stayed, naked and with only their own shit for company.

Some people laughed when the men with the tans pulled guns on them, thinking it was all part of some elaborate interactive entertainment. It was probably called The Violent Hostage Taking Experience. Some of the tourists laughed, admiring the convincing performances of the planted victims when they saw men or women punched or kicked or pistol whipped for complaining that this was hardly a suitable scenario for children, or that they didn't want to play this game. Most people happily complied with the men's demands, went where they were told to at gun point and took their balloons and lollies with them, not wishing to be seen as poor sports or killjoys.

In the Family Plaza, where many visitors had been shepherded along with a few dozen handcuffed employees, there was little to do but mill around in the heat and wait for the joke or fire drill or bomb scare or whatever it was to be over. Soon a heavy bass rumbling attracted the attention of those on the edge of the Plaza, a ground shaking sensation which seemed to be approaching down the Rue International.

Charles Bigger was glad that the Cold War had ended. He'd been able to pick up the decommissioned Soviet tank for next to nothing. People scattered before him as the black painted tank rolled into the Family Plaza and ground to a halt before the hotel. Charles made sure his cameraman got a shot of him looking imposing, low angle, the gun barrel of the tank widening into the foreground left and the squat soft peach cube of the Bigger International rising behind. Within fifteen minutes everything was set up and they were ready to begin.

Charles removed his greasy-brimmed baseball cap, revealing that it conformed all too neatly to the shape of the head beneath, smoothed his hair and squinted his tiny eyes so they almost disappeared. He had waited decades for his cue.

'Ladies and Gentlemen, good afternoon,' he said, reading from the idiot boards being held up beside the camera, 'and welcome.' (STAGE DIRECTION: Raise hand.) 'You don't know me yet, but I'm sure you've all heard of my illustrious grandfather, the founder of the Bigger Amusement World. You're all here because of him, and so am I. I am Charles Bigger. Welcome to *my* world.'

On AmusemenTV all over the park, people could see Charles Bigger's salacious fervour as he looked slightly to the left of the camera, resembling an unassuming but authentically ugly participant in an infomercial about carpet shampoo.

'All entrances to the park have now been sealed. I regret to announce that you are all now my prisoners and hostages, and that the Amusement World is under my total control. You might even call it an independent republic.

Communication with the outside world is no longer possible. And to follow that analogy through, I am its president. That means you have to do what I say. Further instructions will follow. So in the meantime please stay calm,' smiling and making himself look even more predatory, spreading his hands to make himself feel enjoyably Christ-like, 'and don't do anything stupid.'

All heads in the Family Plaza were turned towards the tank from which he emerged like a hideous glove puppet, lacking anything below the waist. The paralysis of shock held sway for a moment; the twilight space of disbelief when the mind flip flops between what it wants to believe and what it knows to be true. And then the sudden sombre roar of thousands of pairs of feet arose as they forgot to be transfixed in spite of their owners' brains. Visitors, day trippers and honeymooners turned without a word and tried to flee the new tyrant of the Amusement World on jelly legs.

Charles leaned into the microphone. 'Make it photogenic,' he said.

The suntans dressed as park security opened fire on the escaping crowd, sharp cracks splitting the air, and sections of the crowd began swerving and changing direction together like hunted gazelles and then someone was hit, the thud of something moving too fast to see being stopped by meat and bone and a collective scream at last went up from the crowd and the first child was trampled and crushed to death as self preservation took over from sense. The tank rolled slowly through the crowd and the carnage so Charles Bigger's crew could get some good shots of the extras in his most ambitious video production to date. A camera flash panned and zoomed in on Maggie Gnu, still in full costume.

She'd been hit by a bullet in the side of the head and there was blood coming out of the little mesh screen over her mouth. She toppled over face down and lay still until she was obscured by dozens of running legs. A young man holding his daughter in one hand tried to drag a handcuffed and headless Marvin Monkey out of harm's way but he fell and was trampled, somebody stood on his face and ran on, oblivious to what she had done. The man with his daughter ran too, dragging her behind him like a broken doll. A woman screamed and screamed as she tried to protect her boyfriend with her own body, pushing people away from the helpless fallen man with weak, futile gestures. It all went out live on AmusemenTV, flickering on every screen in the park, and for the first time the laughing people, the people who could take a joke, knew that nobody was laughing unless they'd been unhinged by shock and it wasn't a joke unless it was of the cosmic variety.

Outside the walls of the Amusement World, the terror and panic were just a dull thunder away off in the distance as ten thousand cars sat baking under the sun in silent rows, empty and forgotten.

(ten)
some meat

Parry drifted along in the drone of machinery and measured his time in the slicing of the bullet train along steel far above his head every 8.5 minutes. He became aware of an itch on his leg beneath the furry costume, and eventually he managed to get the motor power and coordination together to scratch it. His legs tingled as he stood and the blood returned to them. He let water from an unrepaired pipe drip on his face, then lapped at it hamster style without gaining any real relief from his thirst. Emerging into orange light from a door in the base of Mont Marvin, his eyes were appalled by the amber brightness of the sun as it set behind the distant Enchanted Chateau and he realised that he had not been missed in all the hours he must have lain at the bottom of the shaft. He was hurt, but not surprised. Now the park seemed closed and deserted, even though The Amusement World Is The World That Never Sleeps™. He looked up and saw the bullet train dipping into the piranha river, but there were no screams of good natured fear now because the train was empty. The more he looked around him, west to the Enchanted Chateau, towards the shoebox of the Bigger International, behind him down the Rue

International, the more it looked like the aftermath of a neutron bomb attack: the people wiped out and vapourised, but the buildings perfectly intact.

A man appeared some distance away down the Rue International. Parry raised his hand to attract the man's attention, but his voice caught in his throat and the gesture faltered because the man was being chased by four others riding in a pastel golf cart. From so far away it was hard to be sure, but it looked like they were in the colours of park security. One of them pointed at the running figure and the earsplitting report of a gun echoed down the Rue International. The running man arched his spine and thrust his shoulders back, fell on his face and didn't seem to be in any further discomfort.

Parry was unable to make out the expression on the tiny shape's face, but its question mark body told him everything he needed to know. The man was dead, somebody had killed him right in front of Parry's eyes and suddenly everything was wrong. Then Parry fled, really ran this time, took his rabbit feet off and threw them away, dropped his head and left it behind, pounded pell-mell and mindless through the empty streets. When he was a reasonable distance away and certain that he couldn't hear the ominous whine of an electric cart zipping up behind him, he stopped in the doorway of an ice-cream outlet to gather his thoughts and catch his breath, but found himself unable to do either because where were all the people and what had happened and everything was fudge sundae and mint choc chip with vanilla and fruits of the forest with real fruits of the forest flavour and extra thick and creamy with a hint of real vanilla and peach flavour and thick blood red syrup in a disturbing smear down the front of the hygienic freezer cabinet.

Across the road, on the side which was in shadow, four sacks of old clothes lay lined up neatly under a lamp post. On closer inspection the bundles turned out to be people, three men and a woman. Parry knew there was nothing he could do or say but he also knew that their ruined heads and open unfocused eyes would haunt him forever, and so would the way a chunk of rose pink meat had teased itself out in one piece from the side of the woman's head. The four bodies snuggled up against each other on the cooling pavement, all inhibitions long gone.

Not far away Parry found one of the poles which normally bore securicams and the television sets that blared out twenty four hours of AmusemenTV corporate propaganda and noisy cartoons over the heads of visitors. This one looked as if it had been crashed into by a car, and had crumpled over from about a third of the way up. Two of the TVs had been killed in the fall. The third had lost its vertical hold and lay on its side showing the soundless image of a man, his reptilian mouth twisting sadistically as he spoke. The tape loop began again as Parry gingerly reconnected a dangerous looking wire and the PA system stuttered back into life so he could hear the man's voice.

'...understand that you are disposable. I don't acknowledge that you are human beings at all. Give up. Give yourselves up. Report to the nearest hotel. I've killed and I didn't like doing it and I'll kill again...'

The back of the TV sparked and smelled of burning hair. Static on the screen. Something inhuman and evil had got its way.

(eleven)
more meat

They swam across his eyes, strange and beautiful creatures which defied analysis. As he viewed them they folded and unfolded and folded back into themselves again like origami fugitives from a natural history museum display, their textures like bakelite and peeled lychees, their anatomies spindly and hooked and complex. Though they had no faces, their movements betrayed their volition: they moved at different speeds, some with the variegated cadence of the vacillating, others with what could only be interpreted as firm purpose. They cruised silently towards him, skimming across his unnaturally expanded field of vision with the quantized elegance of slow motion playback. Dancing in spirals as the lights went out one by one around them. A pink helix turning, something's coming up the stairs from the bottom of my brain. I can see you. I know your face.

He opened his eyes and somebody was lying on a bed across a blank hotel room. A long, male body, covertly white. A tough sinewy forearm covered in brown hair rested beside it. Another drift of hair on the belly led down to the genitals which, as if composed by a tactful cinematographer, were positioned slightly out of frame. Doggo took all this in during the split second before he realised where he was and that he was looking in a mirror across the room.

He walked carefully towards himself and past to crouch naked before the television which loitered in the corner. He knew about the X-rays, but even turned off it looked lethal to him now. Latent with information. He reached out towards the silent screen. A faint residual electrostatic charge made it crackle faintly as his fingers brushed the warm glassy surface. They passed on, across the screen, along to caress the speaker grille and back around to gently depress the on button.

There was nothing on, as he had expected. Just cartoons, Marvin Monkey rolling around in the mud, getting as dirty as he could and acting insane so he'd be written into his rich aunt's will.

'Are you just proud of your physique, or do you always sit in front of the TV naked?'

Ruthie stood framed in the bathroom doorway with one thumb under her bra strap, halfway through pulling it up over her shoulder.

'Get dressed,' Doggo said. 'Quickly.'

'That's what I am doing.'

'You're beautiful. Do it faster.'

She looked him up and down, smiling.

'What about you? Are you going out wandering in the Amusement World in your birthday suit?' she said, then her gaze moved up to his face and the smile died.

'Where exactly is it we're going to? Just so I have some idea how to dress—'

Doggo frowned, creasing his already corrugated forehead.

'I don't know,' he said. 'Just out.'

'Well how should I dress?'

'Quickly.'

Ruthie got dressed—at her usual speed—and Doggo did the same rapidly. Then he stood behind Ruthie while she did her hair and complained about being rushed. In the end Doggo took Ruthie by the arm like the bouncers who often ejected her from clubs, and physically dragged her away from the mirror. She snatched up her bag as she left.

On the television screen the anti Doggo and Ruthie, the beaming average but good looking family, followed the red carpet into the gaping lobby of the advert land Bigger International Hotel and were greeted with magic. Playing to a vacant room and Ruthie's empty clothes on the bed.

Ruthie and Doggo stepped out of the foyer and into screams bouncing off of the glass hotel front like panicking birds and the bang bangbang of guns firing at random and a confusion of people running in all directions. A woman stopped in front of them and put her hand on Ruthie's shoulder. She looked silently into Ruthie's face for a few seconds, searching for some meaning or explanation there, and neither of them moved until the woman was swept away by the rush of people. Her bleeding hand left a detailed palm print on Ruthie's white teeshirt.

Ruthie, scarcely comprehending how her world could change so utterly from one moment to the next—from one side of a set of automatic sliding doors to the other—ran with Doggo's hand on the back of her head, keeping it down though he knew that neither hands nor speed nor keeping close to the ground made them safe. Only instinct could do that, so Doggo just ran, away from the Family Plaza and the people who had fallen there or were running randomly in circles like wind up toys abandoned on a table top. Instinct might get those other people killed, but he had listened to an instinct which he knew would save them and this was all that was on his brain and in his ears as he ran and held Ruthie's hand tight even though she couldn't really run in the shoes she had eventually chosen to wear.

A few people ran ahead of them in the otherwise strangely deserted street, a page torn from a De Chirico sketchbook, as they approached the outer wall of the Enchanted Chateau and there was a blonde girl at the top of a tower shouting something and waving a carrier bag out of one of the windows. Ruthie tugged Doggo's hand and urged him on with smeared panda eyes, so they never worked out what the girl was saying. Behind one of the Chateau's useless flying buttresses they found an unmarked door jammed shut. The electronic lock was deactivated and Doggo was grateful for all the times he'd gone looking for photographs and disks in people's houses or offices and learned how to do at least some of the things that people expected of him when he told them what he normally did for a living.

In a few long moments they were descending a flight of concrete steps lit by a tired, flickering fluorescent strip that needed replacing. Now they were under the scaffold infested Chateau. They kept looking for EXIT signs, following them in reverse away from the way out until the air started to cool and all they could hear was the humming lights and the air circulating in the ducts. Sometimes they thought they discerned a rumour of distant voices, and tried to head in the opposite direction. Doggo and Ruthie turned left and left and right and left and right and left down white concrete floor corridors and didn't think about where they might be going to until they were so lost that they couldn't even find themselves.

(twelve)
the insects say goodnight

Parry found Maggie Gnu lying dead at the edge of the Family Plaza, her beard and mane matted with congealing blood. He forced himself to work the thing's head loose and look at the human face of the murdered one under the forever happy mask. He felt slightly guilty in his relief that it wasn't Priscilla wearing the costume even though some other poor girl had got herself killed instead, a girl Parry had known slightly but had never really bothered to speak to. He forgot all danger and fear and sat beside the dead girl for a long time, looking at her slack murdered face and trying to work out what to do now that human beings had apparently become as disposable as the paper cups and plastic forks which were being lifted in eddy currents and idly scraped around the plaza as a gentle wind rose and night came.

When Parry heard Priscilla's voice calling his name, he thought he was hearing things again. It took him a while to spot her, but there she was, perched dangerously on the ledge of one of the Enchanted Chateau's fairy tale Gothic windows and waving energetically at him.

It took him nearly an hour to get into the tower, and a while longer for Priscilla to climb down to him the same way she had climbed up, using as hand and footholds the beams and joists that supported the fibreglass façade. Now the sky was dark, and they barricaded themselves in to wait for morning. At the moment there was no escape from the nightmare, but they felt sure that tomorrow someone would come to rescue them and the whole thing would be sorted out.

They sat close and distracted themselves by talking softly to each other about forming a Society for the Prevention of Cruelty to People in Costumes; about how Parry had once wanted to be the actor who played Godzilla so he could get paid to stomp balsa wood miniatures of Tokyo; about how Priscilla had seen a big guy and a tall woman escaping under the Chateau so there must be others running around free and that was good because that meant that somebody would do the Lassie thing and get help; about where they would go if they could go any place they liked and what they would do when they got there. They couldn't think of anywhere and they couldn't decide what they would do.

Once, Priscilla laughed despite everything—or because of it—and though her face was deep in shadow her eyes caught what little light there was and her teeth looked small in her mouth, like cat's teeth.

'Have you ever had an orgasm from laughing?' asked Parry, just for something to say.

'No, but I often got erect nipples,' she said and laughed again, not sure if she wasn't getting a little bit hysterical.

In the end they ran out of words and wrapped their arms around each other until they drifted in and out of sleep, Priscilla's stomach turning over and over and Parry afraid that death was creeping up on them through the beautifully lit stark streets of the Amusement World. The whole kingdom lay silent and inert as Parry and Priscilla sat locked in the fake-looking tower of the Enchanted Chateau and listened to a rubbery matrix of insect voices warping in the darkness.

part two

under the
republic

(one)

erotic machinery, mechanised sex

It was a rare day that went by without a shooting, a garrotting or a stabbing on the Rue International. Brutish meaningless days faded into hopeless empty nights which in turn blurred into the next day and meanwhile the outside world gave no indication that it knew what was happening or could bring itself to care.

Today three middle-aged men had almost escaped from the Amusement World, Charles Bigger's private republic of psychosis. Apart from those who scurried in elusive twos and threes like escaped and feral hamsters beneath everyone's feet in the park's subterranean tunnels, the remaining thousands had been taken prisoner and were securely corralled in the more downmarket hotels huddled in the centre of the Amusement World.

Most of the hotels were stuffed to about five hundred

percent of their design capacity. With the rides and attractions silent, from outside the hotels a constant buzz of voices could be heard. The tourists' cases, bags, phones and cameras were heaped up in plastic skips or just dumped in random piles on the carpet where they had been wrenched from people's hands as they were cattle prodded through the lobby. Further inside, the corridors stank richly of sweating unwashed humanity. The air was stirred only by those who had the energy and the room to pace and wonder why no-one was doing anything. Nobody bothered to bring them food, so after they had eaten the flower arrangements and the contents of the complimentary toiletry baskets, they went hungry.

Charles inspected the shirtless failed escapees, and privately marvelled at their depth of feeling; the stupidity or the fear or the audacity that had made them capable of leaving their families behind and climbing a ten meter high live electric fence.

These men seemed utterly ordinary to him and within an hour he would have forgotten their faces, but he didn't think he had ever felt strongly enough about anything to burn all the flesh from his hands like they had. Perhaps to have control over everything and make all things certain, to lay his bare palms on the beating heart of the Amusement World, possibly for that he would be prepared to risk something. Maybe he already had. But he was not ordinary, and it didn't make any sense to Charles to compare his magnificent feelings to anybody else's prosaic sensations.

They were all thin and haggard, but two of them had kept their age bulging bellies, legacies of the boring sedentary jobs which had paid for their one way trips to the

Amusement World. They had made a token effort to protect themselves by wrapping their hands in their shirts to climb the fence. One of the men had his hands raised in despair or surrender and his skin hung loose in raw flaps from his hands. Another's shirt had been made with some synthetic fibre and was now fused and burnt into his palms in the diamond pattern of the fence's mesh.

Now they were cowed, tired out and numb. Even the man with his hands up hung his head at the futility of it all. Only one of the men voiced a few shrill little screams as Charles's paramilitaries kicked him in the head and the ribs until his lungs split and his brain came out and lay with his broken teeth on the pavement.

Charles grew vaguely bored and wandered away. Already he felt like he had seen it all, had enough of beatings. These days he found himself easily wearied by handguns, primitive knives and saws. He was even fed up with driving his tank around the empty park. The vehicle was slow, the noise of it gave him a headache, and when he had been riding in it he always stank of diesel and had to have a shower. Now the tank was carelessly parked in the middle of the Family Plaza, a militaristic actual size Christmas present abandoned on Boxing Day by a fascist child with attention deficit disorder.

In his films Charles had developed and deployed an extensive vocabulary of torture; drugs, red hot metal, live electrical cables, surgical instruments and scalpels, drill bits and orbital sanders. Now all these props of degradation seemed so peripheral, so trivial. He would let the others play at indulging the vengeful sadisms and gnawing bitternesses which had eaten them up all their lives and led them here to do as they were told and lick at his face for scraps like submissive dogs. It wasn't what he really wanted.

Neither threats nor money had brought to light a blueprint or map of the park's underground areas, the service tunnels and machinery shafts which hummed and echoed just below the daytime skin of the Amusement World. Charles suspected that the place resembled a colony of ants, with only a fraction of itself showing above the ground to hint at the vast extent of the city below. And the ant farm's tacit king, Old Man Bigger, slept in his canister somewhere under Charles's feet as well.

He didn't believe in ghosts but he could feel the tug of the dream Charlie on his waking mind; Charles was a believer in signs and omens when it suited him. The dream meant something. He also read horoscopes, believing every word they said when they were favourable, seeking any reason to ignore them when they were bad.

As a pink golf cart came along to retrieve the bodies of the electric fence climbers, Charles told his driver to take him back to where he had installed himself in the Bigger International Hotel. He thought it highly significant that this building, near the hub of Bigger Amusement World, should bear his name. What could that mean?

There came a distant thin threshing of the air and a speck on the horizon. The sound of a helicopter's rotors.

The arrival of a helicopter meant that somebody out in the world had been alerted to the new regime in the Amusement World. His people were paid well, they were good, knew how to use the guns and electric batons he had provided them with. They had been thoroughly briefed on what to do in such a situation. Despite reassuring himself by running through his instructions to them in his mind, forwards and backwards and forwards again, an oppressive sadness settled on him and refused to go away. He had hoped to at least have a chance to deflect attention with a press conference before they came sniffing around. In fact he had been looking forward to sitting behind a thicket of microphones and smiling, looking into the eager faces of the assembled journalists, the faces that he wanted to smash in with hammers, and fooling the stupid bastards.

Charles looked out of the car window and sighed as the bullet proof glass rolled up in front of his eyes, slicing the sound of the helicopter off and sealing him safely inside. His films never seemed to have discernible endings. Just the sense that they couldn't go on any more, that they had spent all their energy, had run their course and so they ended arbitrarily, more or less as they had begun.

He never wanted this film to end.

encounter with a stick insect leading to painful degradation

Bigger's men had taken to wearing Kevlar-Teflon vests and carrying cattle prods, as if afraid of something. It couldn't be the pitiful inmates of the Amusement World who scared them. Cooped up in their cramped stinking hotels, they had already resigned themselves to daily horror in large doses and to having the prods used on them—sometimes—to keep them subdued.

Parry and Priscilla pressed themselves against the walls of the duct and watched through a grille, once the outlet of an underground staff kitchen, as the armoured men passed overhead without looking down.

Priscilla brushed the back of her hand across her forehead, wiping a cleaner trail through the grime and air conditioner dust. Parry was still wearing Gogo Bunny's ragged and filthy body because he hadn't been able to find any clothes that fit, and he was completely unwilling to consider taking any from the dead chef they found in the freezer behind one of the kitchens. The two of them had been gnawing slick blocks of lard and eating dry muesli out of a huge catering packet when they found the man curled up in the corner, his knees and elbows drawn towards his chest. His body was (a) stiff, but he bore no marks of violence. They decided that he had probably been locked in the freezer when the park was sealed off, or had accidentally done it himself and frozen to death. Priscilla put an empty oven ready chip bag over his head, which she realised was undignified and disrespectful, but she preferred it to looking at the dead man's face.

The two of them had spent the last three hours wriggling through the kitchen ventilation system, with frequent nervous semi-jokes about what would happen to them if somebody decided to turn the fans on. Contrary to what they had imagined, most of the ventilation conduits had not been designed for people to crawl through: the ones that were big enough all either led back on themselves in confusing and laborious loops, or to the surface where Parry and Priscilla didn't dare go. For the first time, Priscilla allowed a fraction of her despair to show.

'They're not going to come, Parry,' she said. 'They're really not coming, are they?'

Her voice echoed down the dull metal sides of the duct.

'Who?' said Parry.

'Exactly. Exactly.'

'Somebody will come,' Parry said. 'Someone has to come. I mean, they can't just leave us all here.'

Priscilla rubbed at a bruise on her bare dirty arm.

'We've tried everything to get out. There's just no way. There is just no way out, and we can't hide down here forever. It's only a matter of time before they catch up with us. Or we do something stupid like crawling into an incinerator or a fan.'

'I thought we were doing pretty well,' said Parry, taking Priscilla's dirt blackened hand in his.

'Parry, look,' she said. 'I've sneaked out of this place in every way that's possible, before now, but these people, they've done their homework and they are not mucking around. They're not going to let us get out of here. Just listen for a minute. Listen.'

Parry tried hard, but couldn't tell what he was supposed to be hearing.

'Listen!' said Priscilla, looking up through the grille. 'Can't you hear those poor bastards caged up there in that bloody Big Head Lodge or whatever it's called?'

'It's the Easter Island Lodge.'

Priscilla looked down at her scuffed shoes.

'Don't be pedantic. I don't want to end up like that, Parry.'

Parry put up his hand to silence her, then put it over her mouth when she protested.

'Can you hear that?'

Priscilla concentrated and she heard it, a dull rhythmic noise which she recognised. It seemed to be getting closer. Without hesitation she reached up and hooked her fingers through the grille, her hands clumsy and hurried, suddenly excited by hope. It only took a few seconds to work the grille loose, and a few more for Priscilla to pull her slim body up and through the opening, too quickly for Parry to make any attempt to stop her.

Parry squeezed through as well and clambered out after her to stand beside the Easter Island Lodge, which had become a surprisingly effective prison with the simple addition of a few rolls of razor wire. It was the first time he had walked in the sunshine since the park had been taken over. Some of the people imprisoned in the Easter Island Lodge had come out of the cabins where they'd been sheltering from the sun to stand amongst the giant grey *moai* which lay in off-the-peg enigmatic positions, half submerged in the unwatered grass. Heads concrete and human stared upwards at the bright yellow helicopter which threshed and sliced the warm afternoon air above them.

Priscilla had already covered quite a distance and was standing halfway down the street, all fear forgotten. One hand shielded her eyes as she looked into the sky and jumped up and down, looking like a deranged, hyperactive cheerleader who had been stuck up a chimney for a week.

The helicopter hovered above the Easter Island Lodge, stirring up swirling clouds of eye stinging dust and dead grass and ice-cream wrappers. There was a man half hanging out of a door in the helicopter's side, waving and resting a hefty camera on his shoulder. Parry strained to hear what he was shouting.

'We're from the TV,' is what it sounded like. 'We're from the TV!'

A snap of gunfire from the top of the Enchanted Chateau, and the screen of the helicopter was suddenly crazed and opaque. The aircraft began to turn slowly on its axis, its engines making an unhealthy sound. Parry grazed his elbows as he hit the ground, shouting something incoherent to Priscilla. It didn't matter because it was drowned by the sound of the whining rotors anyway. Oblivious to everything else, Priscilla continued to wave frantically at the helicopter.

The hidden sniper fired at the helicopter again, his second shot more considered than the last.

The helicopter fell from the sky like a stunned wasp.

Its rotors still turning, it ploughed along the ground, through the razor wire, and embedded its nose in the side of a grassy landscaped bank surrounding the Lodge, which had been designed to evoke an islandy feeling. The people watching from beside the Lodge's drained pool screamed. Spilled fuel and parched lawn took fire instantly.

Priscilla was now lost to Parry behind the thick column of inky smoke rising from the wreckage. He screamed her name again and again but she either couldn't hear him above the cries of the terrified Easter Islanders or was unable to respond.

One man fell out of the crashed helicopter, which now lay on its side in flames, and took a few spastic steps. His hair was on fire. Some people from the Easter Island Lodge tried to put him out with kingsize duvets, which immediately started burning as well and blackened the already choking air with the smell of burning feathers.

Parry heard heavy feet on the block paving and looked up to see three armed men running stiffly towards the Easter Island Lodge, hindered by their bullet resistant vests. By now ragged tourists were climbing over the wrecked perimeter fence, heedless of cut hands and shredded shoes as they scrambled across the razor wire to liberty, either drag-carrying the ones who were too shocked or too injured to move, or pushing them aside in desperation.

One of these people, a girl thin as a stick insect, stood motionless in the middle of a tangle of razor wire. Somewhere along the way she had lost her clothes and was wearing some drapes from the Easter Island Lodge as a poncho, with curtain tiebacks as a belt. The curtains were printed with an ethnic pattern chosen by an interior designer who obviously didn't have any idea of the difference between South Pacific and South America. On her face the girl wore the kind of expression one might expect to find on a person who has just discovered that she is hauling a carrier-bag full of heroin through customs at Dubai airport. A brief change of wind direction allowed Parry to see Priscilla through the smoke, grasping one of the girl's tiny wrists, talking desperately right into her fright mask of a face, pulling her away from the flames. The palm leaves on the roof of one of the cabins were burning.

Parry called Priscilla's name again, told her to run, to get away. All hope of finding her was lost in the confusion of voices, the smoke which was now drifting sideways along the ground and stinging his nostrils and eyes, the jumble of tear streaked dirty faces. Armoured men struck out at tourists with shock batons as they ran past.

A long-faced grey head suddenly loomed out of the black cloud, its eyes obscured and black, gazing blindly out over the shattered shell of the helicopter and startling Parry with its familiarity. As he stumbled backwards, blinded and choked by hydrocarbons and the smell of burning smoke, his foot made contact with nothing and he fought to keep his balance, wobbling on the edge of the duct from which he and Priscilla had emerged.

Someone was staring up at him from the hole in the ground. Shiny sunglasses eyes and a blur of greyness and they were gone, away into the secretive dark places of the Amusement World's workings. Parry knew then that he had to leave Priscilla behind and follow. Hide again and gather the strength to fight his way out of the horror that had tapped them all on the shoulder on a summer afternoon which already seemed to have happened to someone else, a thousand years ago. Otherwise that horror, and the man from whom it emanated, would claim them all one by one, like it had the people lined up on the pavement by the ice-cream outlet and the man trapped inside the walk in (but do not walk out) freezer and the flame haired cameraman and now Priscilla as well. Parry dropped through the veneer of the Amusement World and disappeared.

(three)
wish you could hear

Doggo kicked in the front of the vending machine and hoped that there was nobody around to hear the crack of perspex. He ate chocolate from the machine without really tasting it, each peanut and raisin embedded in the bar a trial to chew and swallow. He hadn't considered it worth the risk to try and get into any of the hotels' backstage food preparation and storage areas, so he had primarily been subsisting on a diet of hyperactivity-inducing children's sweets out of smashed up vending machines, and on pasty raw fries from the Fast Foods of the World Restaurant cluster. What he couldn't eat immediately he stuffed in his pockets and, when he could, threw it to the tourists. Apparently they weren't being fed and were grateful for anything they could get to eat, even if it was always Mini Chocolate Dino Eggs or Big Errs!—Bigger Entertainment officially endorsed real artificial fruit flavour jelly character shapes! (which Doggo was certain must have rankled the tourists, under the circumstances). Doggo's diet of late had left his digestive system hostage to a twin pronged one-two onslaught of indigestion and frighteningly regular bowel movements, but he still considered himself lucky.

Luckier than the poor bastards caged in the Marina Coastal Resort or the Easter Island Lodge like a litter of unwanted gerbils in a pet shop, scrabbling selfishly over each other for the remote chance of a bar of sickly chocolate to eat, or sticking their wrists through the wire as they called out, past putting themselves in someone else's position and heedless of giving him away.

Luckier than the women raped in shifts by delegations from the micro army Bigger had gathered around himself for his audacious little experiment in alternative forms of government. Some—but not all—of the worst psychopaths employed by Bigger were professional mercenaries or hitmen; but all of the mercenaries and hitmen were psychopaths of the most unpleasant stripe. Doggo wondered how many people like that there could be in the world, waiting for the circumstances to be right for their mindless hatred of their own kind, their indifference to humanity, to blossom. He wished there was some substance or process he could use to polish his brain clean of the loathsome crimes he had witnessed.

But all that said, he knew that he was luckier by far than the people who went up to the Bigger International Hotel; the peach clad cube, designed to tower over the park like a benevolent hi-tech giant, now seemed about as reassuring to Doggo as the blood caked pyramid in the town centre was to the average Aztec virgin during a bad harvest.

And he was luckier than poor beautiful Ruthie. Just as the sun cleared the horizon, she and Doggo crept around the Fast Foods of the World Restaurant cluster to forage for the clear plastic sacks full of tasteless sliced burger baps and the huge canisters of offal and filler rich hot-dogs that grew abundantly there. Doggo had quickly learned to trust the buzzing voices at the edge of his consciousness, and had kept them both out of trouble and out of sight since Bigger's coup. He was glad that this crisis had given his instincts such vocal free rein, because Ruthie was more or less dead to the world. She reacted to the whole experience with the faint tolerance that she might have registered in the queue for a late bus or upon discovering that her clothes were still soiled after a trip to the drycleaners. Doggo led her practically everywhere, pushing and pulling her around like a recalcitrant shopping trolley. Mostly she stood still when he let go, and rubbed distractedly at the bloody hand print that the woman in the Family Plaza had made on the left shoulder of her teeshirt. There was a grimy arc of dirt there from Ruthie's perpetual touching of the spot.

Doggo let go of her in the kitchen of the Burger Bin. He told her to stay put, and looked back at her for the last time as she stood amongst the stainless steel deep fat fryers with her hand on her shoulder and her chin on her hand. She was unshaven, but the stubble on her upper lip and chin was soft and insubstantial, only visible at all because of the way the light from the rising sun hit the side of her face. The fryers were silent and cold for once and their oil was turning rancid and cloudy, with a thin layer of dust floating on the surface. Doggo assumed that, like the shopping trolley she had come to resemble mentally, Ruthie could not conceive of going anywhere under her own power. When he came back from the fridge with a bag of damp bread rolls, Ruthie was gone. He never saw her again.

In the lonely days and nights that followed her vanishing act, he ran and re-ran everything they had said to each other and done together until his memories blurred with over-use. The bloody hand print seemed to exercise Ruthie's hands, but it couldn't have been just that. Her mind was elsewhere. Perhaps it was with the girl in the bouncy castle. Some men raped her to death, raped her and taped her a few metres away from where they were hiding and there was nothing Doggo or Ruthie could do. Ruthie had never seen anything like that before, probably not even thought of it. You were so strangely naive and lucky, Ruthie. Wrapped up in cotton wool and somehow never inoculated against all the evil that people did out in the world.

The only time Ruthie ever spoke more than a simple yes or no it was something incoherent about insects and spirals, about the cockroaches not being able to reach her, which Doggo did not understand and didn't pretend to. The Ruthie who had lured him to her palace of nicotine had burst under pressure and hung in ruins like the silicone breast implants of a careless jetsetter.

Doggo did not give up searching for her, or for a way out of the park, and he tried very hard to keep himself optimistic. He crept stealthily through the park's numerous Fast Foods of the World outlets to look for her as often as he dared. But if he was absolutely honest with himself and he had been asked to place his bets, he wouldn't have expected very good odds on a dazed convalescent transsexual surviving in the park on her own.

He returned to the Burger Bin most often, although he saw no logical reason why Ruthie should go back there any more than she had a logical reason to go wandering off in the first place. Through the Burger Bin's smashed plate glass window, Doggo could see the Bigger Pro Golf Course.

Behind the diamond mesh fence a small group of pink skinned men stood around in a semicircle, taking turns to shock themselves with ice cold water from a huge tap normally connected by a hose to the course's intricate sprinkler system.

Doggo approached them cautiously, looking both ways before he crossed the road, and scanning the tops of the surrounding buildings where snipers often hid themselves.

Doggo tried to attract the attention of the men by rattling the mesh with his hands, but they were too busy with their water. He threw half a stale burger roll over the fence and it landed in the middle of the group. The men immediately froze and stared at him, cool water dribbling down their chins and soothing their sunburn. Without taking his eyes off of Doggo, one of them slowly bent down and picked up the bread.

They were even more jumpy than he was, but they didn't call out. Three of them approached the fence on their raw, sunstruck, corned beef legs.

'Have you seen a tall woman? A tall woman, probably wearing a white teeshirt,' said Doggo as they came closer. The three men stopped about two metres from the fence, watched by the remaining three who stood motionless near the now forgotten tap which was leaking away its contents into the parched grass.

'Are you from the outside?' said the one with the burger bap in his hand.

'No,' said Doggo. 'There's no way out, and I've not seen anyone coming in. Have any of you seen a tall woman with dark hair?'

The nearest two looked blank. The third shook his head.

'We buried some people,' he said.

Doggo's heart lurched like an inflatable dinghy with a puncture. He grasped the fence as if he could shake the truth out of it.

'Where? Where?'

'We want to get out,' said Burger Bap, rushing forward so that the mesh was all that separated his face and Doggo's. Doggo took a reflex step back so that the man couldn't grab him. That had happened before.

The other man who had spoken pointed over his shoulder with his dirty thumb.

'On the golf course. There's nothing to see now, though. They've all been buried.'

'We want to get out of here,' said Burger Bap, squashing the damp, grass coated bread between his desperate hand and the wire fence.

'I want to get in,' said Doggo, and began to scale the flimsy fence, which buckled under his weight.

The golf course was empty and quiet, except for the rustling of strategically placed trees and the fluttering of little red marker flags in the holes. The tourists had been drinking its water for days, and already the thirsty greens were beginning to die in patchy yellow clumps.

The men told Doggo where they had filled in the earth over the dead people. He gave them all the chocolate in his pockets. He'd had enough of it anyway. It had melted in the few minutes it had taken him to cross the street from the Burger Bin and climb the fence.

Next to the eighteenth hole he found four bare patches of dry soil, each about the size of a car, slightly heaped and criss-crossed with footprints. Beside the fourth were three black plastic bags. Doggo tipped them out on the green: soiled clothes, odd shoes, forgotten baseball caps, a lost property office display of orphaned personal items. He sifted through the forlorn heaps with his foot. A scuffed red toddler's shoe, with an Ella Fun decal on the upper, divorced from a companion which was probably still on a child's foot somewhere. A pair of blue shorts with an elasticated waist, slit up the front by something sharp. Three twisted pairs of underpants. A grimy white teeshirt with a dark brown hand print on the left shoulder and an overlaid crescent of dirt where somebody had rubbed obsessively at the stain. Doggo squeezed his eyes shut tight as he held the shirt in his hands. Ruthie. Her beautiful face. Gone.

He heard the distant but unmistakable crackle of a voice speaking through a radio. When he opened his sandbag-weighted lids he saw three men in flak jackets emerging from a stand of eucalyptus trees down the fairway, and he did not need to be told that the last thing on their minds was the perfect swing or a faultless hole in one. Doggo forgot the shirt and ran. He wasn't even sure they'd seen him until a shot was fired, he assumed in his general direction. For some reason, a golf course seemed to him to be the most absurd place of all to lose your life; as if death could be graded and prioritised. He headed for the protection of a steep grassy bank, directly ahead. On the other side he lost his footing on the sand and slithered down the side of the bunker on his back. He lay there for a moment, as much stunned by grief and his admission of it even in the face of his own imminent death as he was by his unexpected slide. But his legs would not give up: they wanted to be free.

(four)
the land of hardware

Eight bleached rows of computers conspired at their desks in the dim room. Their blank black screens dingily reflected the burning chalets across the road. Half closed blinds at the windows shredded the flaming buildings' irregular orange light into thin horizontal strips. Three of the computer monitors had been left on, and their screen savers murmured away meaninglessly at empty office chairs.

Parry passed between the regiments of hushed beige casings, a furry ghost walking softly down an aisle of scratchy grey office carpet. He had followed his silent guide through an echoing sewer and up into this building. He was ninety percent sure that was what he had done, in any case. Perhaps he was being towed along, and didn't have any choice but to follow. His saviour, who seemed to have taken it upon themselves to be the Amusement World Sherpa, managed always to remain a blur of movement at the corners of the eyes, a door latch clicking into place, a furtive footfall behind a plasterboard partition. Parry found himself disturbingly unable to convince himself that, in leading him away from the disaster at the Easter Island Lodge, this unknown person could really have meant to save his life if they refused to show themselves to him. But he also asked himself if it wasn't invisibility—the ability to slip through the cracks in the pavement and vanish—which had saved him and Priscilla until today. Invisibility was a survival skill now. A talent for disappearance was something to aspire to. This person, who hovered as ungraspably out of Parry's reach as an optical illusion on a page, was good at that game.

A door at one end of the office space stood ajar, making minute controlled movements on its hinges as if the room beyond was gently breathing. Parry paused a moment, hand on the door, straining for a sound like insects whispering which worried at the periphery of earshot. He took a deep breath and pushed the door open slowly.

He found himself in the rubber skin factory. Its mercury lit silence was broken only by the ambient buzz of the lights and the comfort sound of air conditioning too weak to prevent an odd clash of smells from permeating the room: volatile industrial chemicals overlaid with inert talcum powder and a subtle top note of smoke.

Nothing disturbed the room's hushed inactivity, but many things slept here on rows of polished metal tables.

These dormant figures were the animatronic dummies who lived beside the Park's rides or lurked by the sides of roads and were brought to life by computers and bursts of pressurised air to make frightening, feeble gestures at visitors. A line of disconnected heads sat on a long bench, looking smug and disingenuously innocent. Blank salmon coloured skulls were fused together along ugly seams normally hidden under stiff unconvincing wigs, or were delicately laid open to expose the electronic anatomies inside. A motley herd of stylised African animals, sacked from the Marvin Monkey ride and deactivated, were crammed horn to hide in a corner. They made vague shapes under a single sheet of cloudy plastic.

Parry's new habits died hard, and he kept to the edges of the room, scanning for possible exits or watching cameras.

A robotic doppelganger of Charlie Bigger was propped casually against a wall and looked like he was waiting for a bus which, lacking anything below the waist except a trailing skirt of pneumatic tubes and multicoloured ribbon cables, he would never be able to board. Naked, his skin was an obscene inhuman pink, with no nipples or navel. He was a robot and had neither been born, nor did he have any need for secondary sexual characteristics. Nobody would ever know of his lack because in the normal course of things nobody was brave enough to look. Even so, Parry speculated pruriently about where the dummy's bottom half and groin had been taken and to what purpose. Charlie's tuft of white nylon hair, patently unreal at such close quarters, stood up from his head as if pulled by a force equal and opposite to gravity.

Parry picked up a glassy green motherboard which lay on the bench, attached by a ribbon cable to the robot's insides. He turned it over in his hands, looking at the meticulous binary city of chips and circuit pathways. Charlie Bigger's heart, in the afterlife of celebrity as in reality, driven by logic and fundamentally dead.

Inches from Parry's own, Charlie Bigger's horrible tiny pointed eyes began to scan the room looking for trouble while his square-jawed metal mouth jabbered up and down, all the time making little pneumatic hissing noises.

In sudden shock, Parry yanked his hand away, cutting it on the razor sharp edge of the motherboard. Parry's real heart was beating a rib bursting rhythm in his chest as he looked around to see if the sound had shaken anybody loose. He looked down at his right hand. The circuit board had produced a bloody longitudinal gash along his palm. Painful but not deep, like a paper cut. The robot twitched itself over onto its side and fell inert again, apparently exhausted by its outburst. As he followed the wires that trailed along the table and into the side of some kind of computer control unit, his gaze travelled back to the plastic covered African animals in the corner. Fuzzy mammalian forms pressed random parts of themselves against the translucent sheet. A pointed, bowed tusk and the side of a broad elephantine forehead. The curve of a striped monochrome rump. A domed, milky cranium lurked at the edge of the group, wearing the sheet over itself like a child at Halloween. The antediluvian lowslung snout of a crocodile poked out from underneath the plastic.

Parry turned away from the rejected African automata, nursing his cut hand.

There was a faint rustle of plastic and a scuttle of furtive feet across the concrete floor.

The covering settled back gently over the graveyard of Marvin Monkey's fallen from grace best pals.

Parry swept his gaze urgently across the room, but the person he now knew was in the room with him had hidden themselves in the stillness again. Aware of every minute whisper made by the fur of his costume, he rested his good hand on the cool metal edge of the bench and knelt to look gingerly underneath.

Across the room, two pale bare feet blurred into movement and pitter-pattered away.

Without thinking, Parry clambered up onto the table and began to hop rapidly from one table to the next across the room. When he was halfway there, he heard muted sounds from outside the building and stopped astride two tables. An alarm was cracking the air somewhere outside, and there was the muffled sound of men shouting something he couldn't understand. Parry realised that they must be trying to put out the fire that the crashed TV helicopter had started. He could smell the smoke.

He reached a door which the elusive one must have used to make his escape. It was marked FIRE EXIT. As Parry grasped the horizontal bar, he noticed that it was almost too hot to touch but before the signal from his brain could reach his hands and countermand their action, he had pushed his weight against the bar and the door swung away from him.

The next room was unbearably hot, because it was on fire.

Parry caught a flash cut impression of blue plastic barrels on furious fire, the flames spiralling up in fierce columns to the ceiling. The fire pounced hungrily on the free oxygen in the next room and began to feed.

It licked Parry hard, the tongue of a bitch on a newborn puppy, and it took him forever just to put his arms up by instinct and turn his face away from the killing heat.

Flames surged across the suspended ceiling of the robot factory, and in the shortest moments ever little blobs of molten plastic from the tiles and great showers of exploding light fitting began to drizzle down and stick in napalm blobs to everything in the room.

The automatons' latex skins caught fire quickly and

sagged in liquid white strings over their metal armatures. Skeletal gunmetal bodies lay on their tables in a mass cremation of the dead and crippled cartoon characters, but Parry had never intended to add his own Suttee to their destruction. He was chemical blind and panic stumbling.

He took a lungful of nostril searing blast furnace air and throat shrivelling poisonous black smoke. Then Parry caught fire too.

His bunny suit's funfur patched and warped in the heat as the fire burned Parry's face and hands raw. He felt his skin curl off as it cooked, peeling away layer by layer in the flames, was urgently aware of the sticky burning plastic which couldn't be scratched away as it etched itself deep into his flesh and I wonder where they keep the fire extinguishers in this place...

And darkness covered his face.

(five)

the man with the fish flavoured arm

Priscilla and Stick Insect were about to become cattle on Charles Bigger's private sex ranch. Stick Insect's waxy flesh sizzled slightly when it was kissed by the red hot metal. From somewhere in the depths of her near catatonic state her body dredged up a response and made her vocal chords cry out. She sounded more like a cat struck by a car and left to die by the road than a human being, and Priscilla would have covered up her ears to block out the sound if she hadn't been handcuffed. Charles, a robotically blank welder's mask propped on his forehead, held the blackened wire to the blowtorch flame again.

They were in one of the luxury suites which Charles had requisitioned at the top of the Bigger International Hotel. He had taken over the entire floor and on virtually every wall of every room maps and drawings of the park were taped in haphazard arrangements. The meanings and correspondences of these collages were known only to Charles. Many had been scrawled over with three different coloured markers, in the unmistakable handwriting of a brakes-disconnected destructo psychopath. The floor was strewn with videotapes, a few of them carelessly crushed under a hasty foot or a falling body. Hardcore bondage videos blared out in deranged loops from a bank of television screens against one wall.

Priscilla and Stick Insect were brought up in the lift. Priscilla had not managed to get the girl to divulge her real name, or in fact to do anything at all except make the odd meaningless mewing sound. The aforementioned psychopath spent over an hour microwaving his head on a cell phone, ignoring the two handcuffed women totally as if they were part of the ordinary decor of an expensive hotel suite. Stick Insect curled up in the corner next to the radiator, while Priscilla sat next to her and tried to watch and listen to what Charles was doing without being too obvious about it. He threatened to have someone's fiancé's legs cut off, apparently for failing to come up with a plan of the Amusement World's underside. People were always a disappointment to Charles in some way or another. He often wished he could do without them.

That's interesting, thought some part of Priscilla, the part that could still speak calmly enough to be heard above the constant bass note of terror. He must be talking to someone on the Outside. Interesting, too, how quickly the place she was in had become her everything and the world beyond it had receded so far out of her reach that it had become capitalised.

Charles was little calmer as he made phone calls to his

hired hands who, she now surmised, were infesting the underground tunnels of the Amusement World like grubs in an apple. She worried about Parry, and wondered what had happened to him in the end. She could see the appetite in Charles's eyes, and knew that the totalitarian toy republic he had turned the place into was not enough to satisfy him. Nothing in the world could sate his insane desire, except whatever it was that had been hidden under the Amusement World. She was very much afraid that she and Stick Insect would also prove to be as fatally unequal to the task as the amusement park Charles had coveted for so many years and had now cast aside in favour of some new fixation.

She didn't have time to finish this thought.

Without preamble Charles began to brand and torture Stick Insect. He pulled down his welder's mask to cover his face, wrenched and pulled the girl's skinny legs, marking them deep with hot wire coat hangers. Priscilla could not begin to guess what expression his face wore as he did these things, until he swung up the mask to suck at the crude burns he had made. Then she wished he would flip the mask back down again. Priscilla couldn't watch any more, and turned her face to the hot radiator. She could look away, but she couldn't stop Charles, and she couldn't help hearing or smelling. Each sound of frying bacon and silent cringe of white flesh was like a nine inch nail driven permanently into her brain.

Suddenly Charles swung around, blowtorch still in hand. He lifted the mask off of his head and wiped his forehead with the back of the blowtorch wielding hand.

'You, what's your name?' he said.

'Maggie Gnu,' said Priscilla.

'Maggie Gnu.' Charles laughed, a genuine laugh but a terrifying one in its present horrible context. 'Okay, "Maggie". As much as possible, you understand, well... there was a purpose in this, what I've done, in such a way though a person goes through so much, no... Because a person goes through so much it's possible that a person has to be what you would call... anaesthesia. That's a word from a crossword puzzle. Anaesthesia. You can't do things like I do unless there's some kind of anaesthesia. There's nothing so stupid or revolting that somebody somewhere hasn't tried it at one time or another. But I find that reassuring. It helps. Most people hate the limited menu of thoughts they have to work with. Because most of them have to do with painful memories, obsessions and politically no-no thoughts. Why not be open to them all, that's what I say. Clinical detachment, of course, has always been a good cover for sadism. But,' he shrugged amiably, 'you know...'

He hauled Priscilla up by the chain connecting her handcuffed wrists, and propped her on the edge of the bed, then sat beside her like a concerned relative visiting her in hospital. He held both of her hands. She noticed that his mouth was dry and brown, on loan from a stuffed animal in a taxidermist's window.

'Sometimes you just want to meet a stranger and be totally intimate and tell them all kinds of things. So you can hear yourself and what's in your own heart, because the words are coming out of your mouth for the first time. Tell them all kinds of things...'

He nodded, totally agreeing with himself as he always did. Priscilla just stared, her eyes bloodshot and rimmed with pink. Charles continued, absorbed in his own monologue.

'Sometimes I just lose control and it's like someone else is in the driver's seat for a while. And my mother was just the same in that respect. One night I woke up and she was there, just there like she came from nowhere, with a butcher's knife in her hand and right at that very moment she really really without a doubt intended to cut off my showbusiness aspirations for good, if you know what I mean. Luckily she came to and she just kissed me goodnight and went back to bed. So it must be in my genetics. From that time I thought for ages that grown ups only hugged children because they wanted to kill them.'

He reached up quickly and Priscilla could not help cringing away as he brushed her hair out of her eyes then ran his cold hand across her face like a blind man learning her features. His fingers, hand and arm—all the way down to the elbow—smelled of fish, and she didn't doubt that they tasted of it as well. She didn't want to think about where they had been, so she tried not to, without much success.

'I never set out to go and kill anybody. Do you understand? I wish to make that crystal clear to you at this point. I have never intended to kill anybody. I even liked them. I felt sorry for them. I never wanted to hurt people, I never wanted to hurt anybody at all. Sometimes I covered their mouths to block out the screams. But I was always nice. Would you like some Valium? Xanax, roofies, something like that so you won't feel it?'

A tear hit the back of Priscilla's hand, and her body began to heave and hunch up with soundless sobs.

'I would like you to tell me why you've made people do those things against their wills,' she said, her voice warped by tears. 'I would like you to tell me why this should have happened to me, that I have my rights violated in this way. I would like you to tell me that.'

'I want to be normal so much, but I can't,' he said, and she wasn't sure if he was answering her question, or if he had taken it to be rhetorical. Perhaps he had not heard her at all. 'I've been a spider all these years. I've been a person looking for things. All I've found is sex. A kind of innocence that's fake, violence. It might not be like that for you, or for her or people like her, but for me there's nothing except those things, or at least that's how it appears to me from where I am. I think it's probably because my mother never loved me in any way when I was her child and did something bad. Because she hugged me and wanted me dead. Because they took the park away. I used to love it more than anything when I was young.'

He hardly drew breath when he spoke, allowed no gaps for interjection or thought. Instead he took great gulps at the ends of paragraphs, gasping for air; an eel crossing from one pond to another.

'It's power,' Priscilla whispered. 'It's just power.'

'No. There's no power in it,' he kissed her eyes and she wished she was a snail so she could draw them back into her head where they could not be touched. 'There's only horror. Trying to keep it secret because people don't like it. Like maggots inside a cut.'

Priscilla's shoulders began to spasm up and down again of their own accord and she didn't know why. The laughter just came spewing out of her like a mouthful of sick.

Bigger frowned, the first time he had shown any awareness that she was a living human being. 'Why are you laughing?'

'I'm not. I'm not. There is no funny side to this. Don't you know that thing... have to laugh or you'd cry. It's something like that. I can't help it,' and just as abruptly as she had started laughing, she stopped again.

His hand moved down now and felt the soft muscles of her slender neck.

'I like people. Especially when they're trying to claw their way out of the boot of my car. That's a joke for chrissake. Something to laugh about, if you're a normal person.'

Priscilla wished she had the courage to push his hand away.

'No kind of person would make another person do the kinds of things you have,' she said.

He yanked up her wrists by the handcuffs, as if her hands were disobedient puppies in training. His breath smelled like the insides of old shoes.

He said, 'Listen. I want something to be understood or at least not misunderstood even if it's only once in my whole life. In a way you didn't deserve to be mixed up in such a business. But me and my Grandfather, me and him were always linked together because we were the same and in that way we came to be linked together in violence as well. I understand now that our family was in an anaesthesia, we must have been or things like this would not have occurred. Because all their wounding has gone on in secret places. This thing has helped me to understand that one thing. There's good things about having people scared of you.'

Charles's fingers burrowed their way into her mouth, feeling her tongue. The taste of rancid fish paste in the back of her throat made her gag.

'Please don't do that,' she said (why are you being so polite, he's going to rape you, scream until your throat packs in, John in the tower of the Enchanted Chateau, get out, bite him—)

'I can't help it,' Charles said. 'It's like a French Revolution of the brain. All the servants suddenly become the masters and go mad. It moves up from here and consumes my thoughts, and burns them all away except that one pure thought. It's germinating in me and sprouting up for everyone to see.'

He was scared by himself and his face was white. His eyes didn't look like real eyes, more like they were made of glass. They were shining and he was cold but he was sweating. He turned away from the feeble light as if it blinded him.

She ran for the door but she had not made it to the halfway point before he was hauling her back, and this time there was no weapon for her to use. She tried to scream and he punched her hard on the side of the face. As he looked at her, he rubbed his hands around each other like he was scrubbing up for an operation. He had hurt his knuckles.

'My fingers are paralysed,' he muttered. 'I get this feeling like the ant men are crawling in the middle of my hand and carrying my thoughts away. I'm not here as myself.'

All she could do was lie there on her side, bleeding into the bedspread. She wasn't thinking of how to get away from Charles or out of the room or what was going to happen. She wasn't thinking of anything. She was just paralysed. Looking into his eyes. And nothing, nothing behind them.

Then he pushed her down against the bed, looked at her and he was sweating. He put his chapped lips against her chest, halfway between her clavicle and her breast. She was scared for a long time and then he bit her so hard that she could feel her skin tearing away between his teeth but there was no pain, just shock, just shock. She screamed as it tore.

After that she didn't really have any consciousness of time, only disjointed bits and pieces in front of her eyes as she floated somewhere above the room.

She asked him why he had bitten her. She thought that he muttered something about he got excited. He got excited. But she knew that could not be true and that he didn't feel anything at all.

The taste of salty blood was in his mouth, along with little slippery bits of skin.

He kept on running his hands across her, although not really touching her in any human sense. It was more like kneading dough, as if she was not alive or couldn't feel anything. Pulling her hair so that she moved forward, and biting.

She wanted to speak but couldn't, because she was not there. She bit her own tongue. Her stiff body was in that hotel room. Priscilla was somewhere else or had ceased to exist.

Moving and tearing and biting and finally it began to hurt. His hard hands on her.

The taste of salty something.

She started choking because there was blood in her throat. She didn't know where it came from, but there was so much of it that she started gagging and even though she nearly bit off Charles's lip he didn't seem to be angry. His hands were cold and hard as he held her head in his hands. She would have bitten his mouth on purpose if she had been in any fit state to have thought of it.

Charles made the room a horror room. He knocked her down and she curled up on the floor, tried to keep her head under or bit her own fingers to keep herself from screaming any more.

He started talking to her or to himself again: I feel like I've got no thoughts in my head, I feel like I'm just an animal walking around in the world, why am I doing that? What is it that makes me do that?

Things began in earnest when Charles went into the next room to get his rape kit. The stun gun, the roll of gaffer tape, more wire coat hangers...

Priscilla stared at a rectangular slice of blue sky through a gap in the drawn curtains.

Later his soldiers discovered Charles hiding under the bloody bed in his room, looking wildly from side to side.

'He! He! He! He's been here!' he panted, and would not be coaxed out until they pulled the curtains, put on all the lights, and searched every corner and cupboard.

Priscilla and Stick Insect were wrapped in clear polyethylene sheets, taken down in the same lift which had delivered them to Charles, and dumped in a featureless concrete room under the hotel. Condensation had begun to form on the inside of Priscilla's wrapper, but Stick Insect was already too close to room temperature. She had bitten away the inside of her own lips as she died.

A fly, torpid in the cool basement air, crawled between the plastic and Stick Insect's face, tasting at salty slicks of congealing blood as she went. The fly and her thousand sisters couldn't believe the luck they'd been having in the last few days. There were so many silent fertile places to give birth to their eggs. The fly was sure her children would be beautiful and numerous.

(six)
bringing death to men in slacks

Doggo jogged along the inside of the perimeter fence like a frantic dog at an animal refuge, growing increasingly desperate as he failed to find any hole through which he might squeeze himself out. Behind an artistically arranged clump of fast growing utility trees, meant to blur the boundaries between the Bigger Pro Golf Course and the rest of the park, he found a three storey building, much longer than it was tall. Where the fence joined the curving back of the building he was able to peel open a big enough hole in the golf course's skin to enable him to scrape through.

He zigzagged across a field littered with hundreds of golf balls which had been whacked out from the driving range and then left uncollected, so that now they were half hidden in the unmown grass like a camouflaged invasion of dimpled mushrooms. He only slipped once on a golf ball, but he kept his balance and kept on running.

He leaned against one of a matching pair of slightly larger than actual size fibreglass golfers at the driving range entrance to catch his breath. Their clubs in midswing. Their buck teeth as they smiled white undifferentiated crescents. Their diamond motif sweaters and golfing slacks in smooth rigid folds.

The bullet blew off half of the golfer's hollow head, leaving a ragged fibrous edge not far from the top of Doggo's own. A dark figure swarmed across the gently sloping roof of the driving range.

Doggo ran across the road, jumped a low wall without thinking, and landed hard on his backside on the roof of a canal-side Renaissance house in Venice.

The Tunnel D'Amour offered a jumbled ahistorical float through romantic settings (This Experience is Experienced at Experiencer's Own Risk, Polite Notice Sexual Intercourse is Forbidden Anywhere in the Tunnel D'Amour) which included a virtual Paris with atmosphere but without the French and an Arabian harem with great architecture but without the (whisper it softly) whores, as well as a simulated Venice with polite robot gondoliers but without the stinking algal sewage water.

Rubbery red circular boats normally conveyed passengers seeking cheesy nostalgic notions of lurve through the Tunnel D'Amour's entrancing ventricles. It was impossible to tell whether it was by accident or design that the boats looked like huge red blood cells, clotted now and stranded in the churning torrent of brownish water that still rushed around them.

The settings were entirely reliant upon trompe l'oeil and forced perspective, and were actually enclosed in a long, meandering, high-walled canyon. Instead of wasting time clambering along the fronts of the buildings, Doggo plunged straight into the water. Halfway through the drop he had a fraction of a second to hope that it was nowhere near as deep as it looked from above and that its bottomlessness was an illusion as well. Doggo had never taken swimming lessons, and wished he had got around to it much sooner.

He was relieved to find that the cloudy water came up to the top of his long legs and no further and he began to wade as fast as the water allowed along the middle of the slippery canal, holding onto an underwater guide rail in its centre. Concealed like a troll in the shadows under the baby Bridge of Sighs (which formed the demarcation line between Venice Lite and pre-war Paris City of Love) was a recycler unit which drew water into underground purifiers and spewed it out into another of the Tunnel D'Amour's romantic settings. If the state of the water was any indicator, the machine was more enthusiastic than effective. As he passed under the bridge, the recycler's unexpected sideways undertow caused Doggo to lose his balance.

He was on his hands and knees now. No matter how hard he tried they found no purchase on the slick floor of the Tunnel and there was nothing else at all to hold onto. It was dark under the bridge. Above the waves he caught flashes of a moonlit cobbled square in pseudo France, the Eiffel tower in the wrong place on the Parisian skyline. He felt himself sliding closer to the viciously efficient water recycler unit with every failed grasp and useless foothold. Eventually he couldn't help taking great mouthfuls of water that tasted like it had been percolated through a municipal landfill. His feet slipped backwards and his fingers slid through slime. The machine was hungry. Doggo was an impurity, and it wanted to filter him out.

(seven)
throb

Parry surfaced gently into consciousness, his breath synched to a subdued throbbing, a deep bass vibration in the marrow of his bones. He could not see at first, but the steady pulsebeat of his internal rhythms told him that he was alive. Sometimes they were insistent like a terrible memory; sometimes they lapped subliminally at his drifting mind like some nameless and deeply repressed guilt.

As coherent thoughts slithered around Parry's drifting brain like soap through wet fingers, equally vague faces appeared around him, their bodies nebulous and grey. Carefully they stripped the melted and ragged fake fur away from him. It may have been that he missed huge chunks of what they were saying as he came and went, but they seemed conversationally inept and asked him a lot of strange questions. He wasn't sure afterwards whether or not he had answered them sensibly, or indeed at all. Disturbing spidery fingers brushed against his skin and made him want to scratch. At one point they held him down gently on a soft horizontal surface—there was no need, he could not move—and inserted something narrow and rubbery into his nose and down his throat. It didn't hurt at all but it gave him a slight nosebleed, which as he was lying on his back left him with stinging sinuses and a metallic taste in his mouth similar to biting on aluminium foil. He drowsed through a laborious form of surgery which took many hours and might have been excruciating were it not for the fact that his awareness of his body was limited to occasional and random flares of indefinable sensation. They meticulously replaced his burnt off eyelids. He felt raw and itchy all over and was too afraid to move, even if he had been capable of it, in case he split out of his skin like a sausage stuck with a fork.

Later Parry was able to open and close his eyes of his own volition instead of having the eyelids held between delicate fingertips, and the third time he tried it he found that his vision had cleared slightly and he could actually see again. He raised his head. It was curtains pulled dark. Vague shapes loomed at the edges of his perception and would not come into focus.

The thing regarded him calmly with bulbous, oily black eyes. It peeled itself away from the shadows and approached him with neurotic, insectoid movements.

'Okay,' said Parry. 'Now I have gone utterly insane.'

As the thing twitched closer to Parry its previously schematic face grew less diffuse and took on more definite form. The pear-shaped head seemed luminous, as if lit from within. Its bulging cranium had a waxy sheen. Pale skin the texture of worn suede stretched tight over it.

'Can I get up? I'm not going to open anything up or do myself an injury? You're not going to hurt me if I get up, are you? Can I get up?'

It gazed at him as if to say, I don't know, *can* you? and Parry saw himself reflected in its black goggle eyes, which never blinked because they had no lids.

Parry's face and hands were pink and smooth, the skin scrubbed and new. His hair felt fuzzy and fine, as if it had been washed too often or cut from a baby's head and stuck to his with Pritt.

The grey fur of his rabbit suit was clean and looked like it had been lovingly and methodically brushed. In fact it felt cleaner than when Parry had inherited it from the Amusement World's costume department. The outfit's seams had been clumsily sewn with some thick ropy fibre in gigantic ungainly loops, made by giant childish fingers for a human sized doll to wear. Parry itched inside the suit, and rubbed distractedly at his skin through the second furry one on top. Perhaps it was being clean again after so long which felt strange.

'You are not insane, Parry,' the insect thing said, its voice like kicking a pile of damp autumn leaves, a memory of cooling radiators as they settled in the night, a voice wrapped in layers of tissue paper and packed in polystyrene chips.

'What are you?' said Parry. He noticed the regularity of the tiny hairs embedded in the backs of his hands as he never had before.

'We conveyed to you information that contact would be re-established after a fire,' said the thing.

'You!' said Parry. 'It was you. Who the hell are you?'

'It is possible that you, Parry, are familiar with the concept "avatar",' said the creature, pronouncing the inverted commas so clearly that Parry could almost see them hovering in the air between himself and it.

'I don't know what you mean,' said Parry.

'Avatar. Manifestation in physical form.'

'No,' said Parry.

'Three dimensional cross section of individual being in this time and place moving forward in a linear manner.'

Parry shook his head.

The thing, sexless creature, extended all three of its fingers to make prongs for poking forward.

'You, Parry, are putting your fingers through a sheet of glass.'

'Am I?'

It shook its head, obviously a gesture picked up second hand, the product of book learning. It was more like the bobbing of a helium-filled balloon on a string than a movement resulting from the interplay of impulse and nerve and bone and sinew and blood in a living being.

'No. Analogy. Resembles. Is like.'

'Where have you taken me? Who are you? You, avatar, whatever your name is, I'm talking to you. What do you want?' said Parry. These questions the tip of a huge drifting iceberg of inchoate others with no words or structure attached to them yet.

'This room unfolded for purpose of meeting. Encounter. Rendezvous. Name is arbitrary label,' it said, reading his mind and forming his questions for him. 'This avatar extended for purpose of mouthpiece. Delegate. Agent. You, Parry, are also agent.'

'I know what you remind me of now,' said Parry. 'You remind me of junk mail. The kind where your name is filled in by a computer on a pre-printed letter. The kind you don't ask for.'

'Name is arbitrary label. You may, Parry, choose one if

you wish to refer to me by arbitrary label, according to conventions of popular fiction, cultural preference or personal comfort.'

The creature began to stalk gently away on legs which looked like they had been broken along their entire length and then left to heal on their own. Parry followed cautiously behind, scratching at his itchy chest and the parts of his back that he could reach, feeling tender and slightly hungover. Parry was far too preoccupied to notice the decor, but the room crept along imperceptibly to follow them, filling in detail as it became necessary.

'Don't aliens have names?'

'Not aliens. Indigene. Aborigine. Native. We have been here longer than mammals, vertebrates. Empire of insects. Kingdom of angels. Species X. Connected. Earth computer.'

'So what about the saucers? I saw them. I've seen you up there, you know. Was that you?'

'Our ubiquity omnipresence is our invisibility. Insects everywhere. Sometimes you see us, Parry. Primates like you see us or we choose to project agent and primates see us or we communicate things that are necessary. Quote flying saucer unquote is a part of us. Organ. Component.'

'Why did you come here?'

'You, Parry, came. In terms of linear time. Not us.'

'I'm sorry. I'm sorry. I'm just trying to hold onto my sanity here. Aliens and everything. You didn't answer the question.'

'For places like this we come,' said the avatar, pointing a thin finger upwards, and they had somehow made their way into a damp concrete place that Parry recognised, somewhere under the Amusement World.

'To tap into interesting cerebral processes, live with you. And in addition to redirect you, some parts of us do that, yes. We admit that to you and it is not necessarily a source of agreement between us.'

'You mean you farm us,' said Parry. 'You're using the Amusement World as some kind of twisted farm. It's like an ant farm to you.'

The thing's body did not move a muscle (if it even had any) but its voice seemed in some indefinable emotionless way to shrug.

'You build yourselves into "ant farms" your term.'

It pointed towards Parry, and he looked over his shoulder. Just to check that the creature was not indicating something even more frightening than itself standing behind him.

'It is not possible that some things are told. You, Parry, must meet us,' it said.

'Okay,' said Parry, 'I'll meet your little friends if you want.'

On an impulse Parry reached out and took the creature by the hand. It did not seem surprised, and didn't move or react in any way except to fold its pencil thin fingers gently around his, which were cold. Its flesh was dry and spongy to the touch, with a uniform consistency which reminded Parry unavoidably of car upholstery. And its skin, if that's what it was, seemed to be at precisely the same temperature as the room; almost as if it wasn't there at all.

'Just one word: anaemia,' said Parry. 'Get yourself some iron supplements, ghost boy.'

(eight)
insect POV

'Parry, you sometimes walk above conduits and pipelines and do not know of their existence,' said the grey avatar. 'Air vehicles pass through flight corridors above you and you do not hear them or know where they are going. Radio television microwave satellite communications and transmissions of information are passing through your body without your knowledge. Electromagnetic fields invisible to the naked or human eye.'

Parry's insectoid companion was trying to explain to him about the nature and existence of its kind. It was answering all of his questions, spoken and unsaid, but it was answering them all at once and not really helping.

The avatar told him of the invisible hand and eye of the Hive; the mind from which entities of its kind wrenched themselves away, like ambitious autonomous fistfuls of plasticene from some great homogenous lump, to come into the world. The true Hive Mind, that was made of them all and into which they faded when they were finished. It was the working of the mammal mind made pure and complex, its primal mother, where the lines of demarcation between actual and imagined memories blurred. Three thousand years ago the Sumerians called them Maskim when they extruded themselves into the real. Named them Ensnarers and feared them as the worst of all classes of demons. Before that, in the Dreamtime, humans knew the agents of Hive, recognised them for the arbitrary gods that they were and drew spirals on rocks in remembrance of their terrible beauty. Primate Mind, searching for certainty and afraid of it, fearing the Hive Mind, sea of shifting relevant-irrelevant information. All this and more, pounding on Parry's ear drums and going into his memory without him necessarily understanding what it all meant or hearing it fully.

These pieces of information lodged somewhere in his brain like swallows under his eaves to wait for their season, when they would take flight and their true magnificent purpose would be revealed.

'We are the conduits under the world,' the creature said. 'We are flight corridors, we are invisible transmissions. You require special equipment to receive us.'

Parry walked along for a few moments with the thing's dry hand in his, wondering what would happen if he never let go.

'Is that a roundabout way of saying you're an elusive little bastard?'

The insect did not reply.

The creature led Parry into a white room, its tiles crazed and cracked, its grouting dark grey and brittle with age. A dusty dim lightbulb hung on a length of flex through a ragged hole in the high crumbling ceiling. Parry followed the cable up into the darkness and could not see its end. Rectangular sepia ghosts of long gone fittings and furniture traced the walls. A floor the colour of fresh blood sloped gently downwards to a discreet drain in one corner.

'So where is it?' said Parry. 'Where is this thing?'

He was strangely disappointed. Now more than ever in his life, he knew that assumptions and expectations had lost all purpose and meaning, but what had he really expected? A shining insect oracle; a giant, hypertrophied, pulsing brain in a tank of nutrient fluid from a Fifties Sci-Fi paranoia flick; a sense of being ushered into the presence of the hallowed; a sacred tabernacle of chitinous wisdom; a holy beehive, its waxy cells manifold and incessant; a hidden crypt for the dead dry husks of the avatar's forebears stacked in hexagonal niches. What he had not expected was this Marie Celeste clinic with the tiles dropping off of the walls and its pitiful remnants of prosaic human use in the dim past of the Amusement World, before it was stripped and sealed off so that only those inspired by madness or focused by obsession might find it. The thought of it made him itch.

He didn't understand.

'Minds are not found on maps blueprints topographies, Parry,' said the creature, and the ping of the bulb extinguishing itself sang out loud in the tile-hushed room.

Parry stood totally still in the perfect timeless dark and waited for something to happen.

He felt something sweep past him in his blindness. It was a sensation somewhere between the physical shock of wet hands on a light switch and the inward mental lurch that comes with news of a death in the family.

Parry instinctively put his hands up in front of him and could not see them, even in his imagination. Now he could feel the closeness of something huge and a placelessness, as if the room itself had grown massive to accommodate whatever was approaching and its walls had withdrawn in awe.

The thing's proximity a dynamo electric hum.

Parry's hair standing on end with electrostatic charge and the primate fight or flight instinct written deep in his head telling him to run, but a voice on top of it saying where to? Where will you run?

Something deathless and ancient in that room with him, terrible with energy.

Parry reeled backwards, staggered and fell hard onto his knees and forgot to bruise them as he saw. He saw everything at once. A blur of images, a torrent of throughput, random pictures nicked from Stevie Wonder's photo album. All the things that the avatar had told him in words, now made flesh and sense and more. The sum and the synergy of countless billions pastpresentfuture who had lost themselves to Hive Mind in hubristic error or rapturous epiphany or accident coincidence if you can believe in that kind of thing after all you've seen in your very short life. Origami folding senseworld faceless endless DNA helix turning. He saw things from an insect's point of view. Hierarchies of organised intelligences, immaculately sculptured machinery, interlocking in precise geometries and yet viewable from all angles simultaneously, everything turning and slotting and sliding in directions unknown to the human senses. The loss of one meant nothing here. It was no more painful to this multitudinous mass of mindless non-thought than a single pebble taken home from a beach in the pocket or a solitary blade of grass plucked from a lawn. Here everything that anyone was could be absorbed and they were unafraid of extinction because there could be none, not here—

And Parry fought as he had never fought anything ever before in his path-of-least-resistance life and refused to be lost inhuman to the Hive. He would not be effaced out of existence. He would not go to nothing. And Parry knew then that the opposite of knowledge was not ignorance but deceit and fraud. That solipsism was not without its benefits, but it was not a very safe place to hide. That none of the things which had gone before had happened because Charles Bigger, mythic monster boy, needed his own private S/M playground. Bigger had been pulled, like they all had, by the invisible chunks of circumstance, heredity, sickness, history, which had ground against each other and locked into place to form the intricate, infinite nexus of machineries that had brought them all together in this place.

Then Parry's mind was alone and he was just listening to himself think, but he soon realised that it was not him thinking any more.

It was someone else entirely.

(nine)
in the presence
of the icon

Parry heard the sound of his own quickened breathing again and felt the chill of the concrete floor hard and painful beneath his tender knees. He took his hands away from his eyes and the room was exactly as it had been seconds or days ago. The furniture marks on the wall. The drain clogged with broken tile fragments. He screwed his eyes up against the glare of the urine coloured light from the bare thirty watt bulb which dangled over his head. He watched as it swung in tiny diminishing circles until it centred and hung still.

When his eyes had acclimatised themselves again to the room's murky light, another feeble source of illumination was visible through the dirty circular hospital windows of a pair of undercoated grey swing doors he hadn't paid much attention to before. Pushing the rusty hand plate of the left door, he passed through into a long echoing corridor. Big enough to comfortably drive a car down, but otherwise dark and featureless, except for a slit of yellow brightness at its opposite end. As he got closer he saw that this light was escaping through sliding doors the colour of orange squash, which stood teasingly ajar. He leaned against one of the huge metal doors, and after a few seconds it moved aside with a grinding protest that set Parry's teeth on edge. He slipped through the gap and into the Amusement World's dead secret heart.

The place was like an aircraft hangar in cement, its vaulted ceiling receding by degrees into invisibility. Bulkhead lights did a better job of illuminating the walls than they did the room. Those lights which had not burned out were dusty and flickered erratically. The damp air smelled of long dead cats and entombment, of decades long burial in airless soil and liberated ozone from broken fridges. From somewhere in the darkness came the steady drip of a trickle of subterranean water working its patient way through the silo's roof.

But the overwhelming presence in the room was the foreground tidal pulse of coolant pumped through pipes and an echoing syncopated buzz which issued from dozens of bulky refrigeration units. These pipes and conduits radiated outward from a dull stainless steel canister in the centre of the room. The container resembled an ordinary tin can, but scaled up in every dimension and detail, right down to the lid which might have been cut around its circumference and peeled up by a gigantic tin opener. In front of it a surgical looking table on wheels lay on its side, as though abandoned by a hospital joyrider who had taken it out for a spin.

'Are you still here?' said Parry.

The Hive Mind's avatar either didn't think the question should be dignified with a reply or had nothing to say; expressionless as ever, it lurked small and strange beside the silver cylinder.

'Well,' said Parry as he stood by the orange doors.

'What am I supposed to do now?'

The thing slowly moved its bulging head towards its virtually non-existent shoulder to make an unreadable gesture which might have been a shrug or an admission of ignorance.

'We can explain nothing,' it said. 'We ask you to believe nothing. But in what we have just shown you and in what you are about to see lies the answer to everything that you ask.'

Parry scratched at his scalp through his hair, frustrated and shaken. Scared by the suspicion that he had left the world he lived in before and that he might not ever be able to get back to the way things were. Scared by the fact that the idea of it excited him.

'But I didn't understand most of what it was trying to show me,' he said.

'The Hive Mind is ancient old enigmatic,' said the insectoid, at least looking if not sounding almost embarrassed. It had the air of a long suffering teenager accompanied by an eccentric and flatulent relative to a school disco. Or perhaps Parry was just trying to make the thing more human by imagining that it felt or saw the world in any sense like he did.

'You're telling me.'

'It still talks today now on occasion,' it said without taking a breath. Parry realised that he had not once seen or heard it breathe. 'But it is so worn thin and out that very few can understand what it is saying.'

'Sounds sweet,' said Parry.

'You, Parry, only brushed against its edge. It can kill the unwary unwilling unwanted.'

'So what is this?' Parry said, trying to trace the tangle of heavy cables and tubes back to their respective refrigerators and generators.

'The cryonic chamber of Charlie Bigger. The founder creator icon of the Amusement World.'

'I know who he is. There's robots of him all over the place. He's alive, then?'

'No,' it said.

It tapped an antique looking dial, which started doing its job again with a glassy little squeak.

'He is quite dead. But preserved. In here.'

It placed its hand against the metal, then pointed to the middle of Parry's forehead.

'In here.'

Parry started feeling his way around the canister's frigid casing, trying to find some hatch or window so that he could see in, and leaving five shiny slug tracks with his fingers on the dusty metal.

'I heard rumours about this. You know, that Charlie Bigger thought one day scientists would find some way of bringing him back. So the old bastard could terrify everyone again and spend all the money he made. I didn't think it was real, though. I thought it was just a story. And he's still here, after all these years. Hasn't anybody ever tried to move him? Bury him or something if he's dead. I don't know… something.'

'This is what his grandson really seeks. Psychic resonator,' said the thing, meeting him on the other side of the canister without appearing to have moved.

'What?'

'Psychic resonator. Locus or focus of real unreal. Half in

your world and half in ours. You had no substantiation evidence proof Charlie had done such a thing, but wished to believe it could be so. Forgotten notorious it holds onto the human imagination. Oscillates between what it is and what it represents.'

'Because they forgot. Because they forgot where they put the old bastard. Or they couldn't be bothered to remember in the first place. I suppose it never occurred to him that nobody would want him back,' said Parry.

'That is correct,' said the insect. 'Because those that came after Charlie Bigger made him into the thing he has become. Icon. Now his corpse has powers properties real and imagined together indivisible. Because his grandson kills for it and approaches enters violates our realm, Charlie Bigger and we become more real. Because secrets need darkness in which to multiply breed grow.'

'So what you're saying is that Charles Bigger has done all the things he's done, killed and raped and murdered people, taken over the whole Amusement World just because of this... because this old stiff in here put some kind of spell on him?'

'No,' said the thing, 'Because Charles Bigger is a megalomaniac insane Stalin delusions in his brain and because chain of events made it possible. Psychic resonance or "spell" your term is incidental, Parry.'

'If it's all about Bigger, what do you need me for?'

'Depicted as emotional need,' said the thing, 'In fact want.'

'Okay, but you did a nice thing. You did good. You're capable of that, even if he isn't,' said Parry.

The thing grew eyelids and blinked hard.

'We do not last four hundred million years into past and future because of values, Parry. We quote prefer equilibrium stasis adherence to way things are.'

Somebody approached out of the darkness, their footfalls both amplified and deadened by the huge space. The figure, coming towards Parry across a slick of lush green algal slime that thrived on the drippings from a corroded pipe, slowly resolved itself into the thin form of Priscilla.

Parry didn't say a word, but skidded urgently across the slimy floor to her and held on to her tightly, feeling the utterly real pressure of her body against his fur, and the tender skin beneath, and a kind of mindless joy that he still had something factual and unquestionably real to hold on to.

Priscilla didn't say anything either, just stood there with her arms squashed by her side, looking bewildered but clean and unhurt.

'I thought I'd lost you,' Parry said. 'Where the hell have you been? Are you alright?'

'Well, I feel like I've been sitting on a very hard bike seat for about a week,' said Priscilla slowly. 'But I'm fine, all things considered.'

Parry lifted up her arm. He remembered distinctly that there had been a yellowish brown bruise on her forearm when he had looked at it in the duct under the Easter Island Lodge, and the way she had stood there rubbing it when she despaired of the two of them ever getting out of the park. Now her arm was not only scrubbed, but unblemished as well.

'But where have you been?' he said.

'I've been with you all day, Parry. I just went to have a look around.'

'No, you haven't been with me. Do you remember the

helicopter at the Easter Island Lodge? And the girl? You helped a girl. We got separated. The people escaping over the wire. From the Easter Island Lodge. Do you remember?'

'Of course I do, Parry. What is your problem? I'm fine.'

'What about the girl? The thin girl.'

'I don't remember... no... was she wearing a plastic bag... on her head? I don't know. Perhaps I imagined that. I don't remember any girl.'

'Where did this come from, then?' said Parry, pointing to a long vivid dribble of recent blood down the front of her shirt. He noticed that although her face and hands looked like they had been on the receiving end of a good wash, her clothes were still as grimy around the cuffs as he recalled them. She looked down at herself, bewildered.

'I suppose I must have had a nosebleed,' she said, putting her forefinger up each nostril in turn to check for evidence of an event which she obviously didn't remember.

'Where have I been then?' said Priscilla, repeating herself when he shrugged, still probing her nose. 'And what's this thing?' Her attention switched from the mysterious blood to the silver container. Like Parry, she felt compelled to walk around the thing and put her hands on its surface. She drew her hand back sharply, then touched the cylinder more gently.

'It's cold. What's it for? What's inside it?'

'Apparently old man Bigger really did have himself preserved in a freezer when he died, if you can believe that,' replied Parry.

'I can believe a lot more than I used to,' said Priscilla, inspecting a row of dials as if she had the slightest idea what their needles and numbers signified. 'He is dead though, isn't he?' she said.

'Who's to say?' said Parry. 'He might be dead, or floating in here in his own little dream world.'

Priscilla picked the surgical trolley up and set it back on its wheels. She sat cautiously on it and then began to slowly scoot herself across the floor with the tips of her toes. Its wheels squeaked slightly as they turned under protest.

Parry stopped the trolley with both hands and looked hard at Priscilla.

'Are you sure you're really okay?'

'I'm okay. I'm just thinking.'

'What about?'

She avoided his gaze without really knowing why and inspected her feet as they dangled just above the green blooms on the grey floor.

'Did you know that there were deer in the Amusement World? I didn't think there were any animals in the place that weren't robots, you know—real animals. But I saw some deer. Funny looking things. Grey, not like the kind you see in pictures. They didn't look how I imagine a deer would look, anyway. They had these beautiful eyes, these beautiful big black eyes and they just seemed to stare at me the way an animal stares into a bright light. Not afraid. Looking at me. They must have escaped from somewhere. Did you ever see them, Parry?'

She looked up at him then and frowned.

'What the hell are you smiling about?' said Priscilla. 'None of this is particularly funny, you know.'

'I know what you're talking about. You're talking about one of these things that I've been talking to. They aren't deer. They're here to help. I think they are, anyway. It's kind of hard to tell. Mr X, avatar, whatever your name is, I completely forgot you were here—'

Parry looked behind the canister and beyond the orange doors. Even the creature's tiny footsteps had evaporated.

'You did good,' called Parry to the darkness. 'You bloody liars. Equilibrium my arse. I know you did a good thing and I won't forget it. I've got the message. I'll pass it on.'

The thing silently fuzzed back into the shadows from which it had been born.

(ten)
scars

Priscilla and Parry looked out over a becalmed and apparently endless black sea that had never seen daylight. Concrete pylons strode away across it and disappeared into darkness under a low ceiling.

They had guided themselves by touch, up a slippery and lightless spiral staircase which rose from the far end of Charlie Bigger's crypt, following the smell of thousands of gallons of stagnant water until they emerged onto the steeply sloping cement beach where they now stood. A smudged brackish line near the top marked the high point of a massive swelling of the reservoir's contents at some time in the distant past. Behind them the walls curved gently away in both directions.

They were about to turn and grope their way back down the steep staircase when Parry shushed Priscilla and they both froze like nocturnal animals in a flashlight.

Something was sloshing slowly and methodically through the water in their direction. As the thing's white form, of gigantic proportions, came closer and reared up from the water they saw that it was not refraction that made it huge. Parry and Priscilla hopped and skidded down to the water's edge to help the man struggle through his exhaustion and up to the top of the concrete slope. He was wearing the tourist uniform of teeshirt and shorts but didn't have a tan and looked in every way completely unlike the average visitor to the Amusement World.

'How did you get down here?' said Priscilla.

The man looked up at her with piercing black bloodshot eyes, framed by the heavy stress lines that Priscilla would have seen on her own face in a mirror.

'I lost someone,' said Doggo.

'Someone you came to the park with?' asked Parry, rubbing at his belly through his furry suit.

'Yes, well... no, not really. I was looking for her. Her name was Ruthie... she was definitely a someone, though.'

He appeared to be on the point of saying something else, but he closed his mouth again. The big man looked so utterly desolate and profoundly vulnerable as he sat silently against the wall for a long time that it didn't seem right to disturb him.

After a while, he seemed to decide that he had turned the grief or remorse or whatever it was over in his mind for long enough and had looked at it from every possible angle. Doggo turned his attention outward again, and studied them both minutely, provoking a slightly alarming and subtly physical sensation in Parry, similar to being X-rayed. He could see that Doggo's mind was riffling backwards and forwards as slowly and overtly as if his thumb and finger were moving along a drawer full of files, trying to remember where it was that he knew Parry from. That was the disconcerting thing; Parry had never to his knowledge met this man.

'Perry,' he said, after a few moments.

'Parry. How did you know that?' said Parry.

'You're the one who plays Gogo Bunny, aren't you?' Doggo answered, as if everything was self explanatory. It wasn't.

'I'm still none the wiser,' said Parry.

'I have to admit... the fact that you're wearing his body is a slight clue, as well. And *you* were hanging out of the window of the Enchanted Chateau the day it happened.'

'You saw me,' said Priscilla.

'You're lucky none of Bigger's men did. Good hiding place, though.'

'Uh... thanks.'

Then they introduced themselves to each other properly, fully aware that it was slightly ridiculous to be making polite introductions after everything that had happened to them all, as if they were guests at a genteel soirée instead of two fugitive cartoon characters and a half drowned semi-unemployed detective.

Doggo explained his job as a mystery tourist and his clandestine observation of virtually all of the cast and staff at one time or another, at least until they started to be sacked and replaced by people who, with hindsight, must have been Bigger's murderous sleeper hitmen posing as the ubiquitous rubbish collectors and burger flippers. Priscilla asked Doggo if he had ever reported her for activities contrary to the spirit of the Amusement World, and Doggo told her that he didn't believe that to be the case, but that he had been known to be wrong before, so the two of them got on reasonably well with each other from the word go. Priscilla couldn't tell either of them very much that they didn't know already because, to her visible frustration, her memory suddenly seemed to be filled with holes at crucial points. Parry told them about the saucers he had seen, and once he had started he couldn't stop himself and rapidly reeled off everything that had happened to him in as near to chronological order as he could manage; the fire in the automaton factory and the avatar, the deaths of the TV people and his visionary experience in a room somewhere below them. Throughout all of this Priscilla looked either sceptical or confused but didn't say a word; Doggo was silent as well, but nodded now and then as if it was all making sense to him. When Parry got to the part about Charlie Bigger's preserved body in the chamber below, Doggo interrupted to tell them what he knew about the life and death of Charlie Bigger. As Doggo spoke Parry could clearly visualise myths on top of rumours on top of desires, all laid down in layers which he could now read as easily as a geologist could examine the countless strata of an ancient rock formation and instead of seeing a gravel driveway of the future, could envisage ancient floods and extinctions, and the periods of equilibrium and inertia which followed them in turn.

It was an open secret in certain circles that Charlie Bigger had spent the last few years of his life as a paranoid and demented troglodyte, obsessed with his own assassination and holed up away from the reality of the world above. He finally entombed himself far beneath the kingdom of recreation which he had made from nothing and waited for death. What was less widely known was that the "Charlie Bigger" who had lived into his eighties and died in a golf cart collision on the surface was a lookalike recruited on the real Charlie's behalf by his son to keep the company together and maintain the buoyancy of its shares on the stock market.

Considering Charlie's avowed and avid anti-Semitism, it was an irony of grotesque and gigantic proportions that Donald Bigger's lackeys came up with a Jewish accountant to take the old man's place. The most skilled and least principled doctors of the day performed primitive plastic surgery on the forever nameless bookkeeper—in specially constructed operating rooms inside the walls of the Amusement World itself—to heighten the resemblance. The doctors then became the victims of contracts taken out on them by Bigger's son, as did the unwitting accountant's family. Despite all his murderous efforts, the Amusement World soon slipped through Donald Bigger's feckless, supercilious fingers and into the greedy crusher of multinational ownership. Within six months Donald Bigger was hanging by a piece of official Amusement World merchandise from a light fitting, there to be found by his young son: Charles.

When Parry and Priscilla asked Doggo how it was that he knew all this, he seemed surprised; he had always assumed that it was more or less common knowledge, like Marilyn Monroe's political murder or the madness and death of the vampire Ceausescu. Parry supposed it was the same as him (or Charles) hearing from some ill defined and forgotten source that Old Man Bigger was preserved somewhere under the Amusement World. Or perhaps it was just that Doggo moved in more glamourously Machiavellian circles than Parry did.

When the three of them had talked themselves out, they

sat quietly by the light of a single lightbulb, throwing pieces of broken concrete into the reservoir below and watching the concentric perfection of the ripples as they expanded across the surface and dissipated.

Parry suddenly rolled back onto the floor, rubbing madly at his right arm.

'Parry! What's the matter?' Priscilla took his hand, while Doggo stood uselessly by.

Parry continued to worry at his arm, trying to work his hand down inside the collar of his rabbit suit.

'It's driving me insane,' he said. 'It's driving me mad. I've been itching ever since the fire. I can't stop scratching. It itches so bad. It feels like there's something inside this suit. Have you ever had a broken arm or leg, had a cast? That's what it feels like, like an itching under the plaster that you can't touch. Shit!'

'Perhaps those things gave you... something,' said Doggo.

'Like fleas,' said Priscilla.

'No, I'm serious,' Doggo said. 'Perhaps they've got diseases.'

Parry cried out in abject irritation again.

'Help me,' he said, clawing at the back of the suit. Priscilla made him turn around and fumbled under a cleverly designed, almost invisible seam which concealed the costume's zip from curious eyes. When she had found it, Parry yanked it out of her fingers and pulled it down, quickly wriggling his arms out of the bunny suit. In the moist dead air, Priscilla's sharp intake of breath seemed absurdly loud. Doggo took an involuntary step forward, his hand half raised in a feeble pointing motion. Parry completely forgot to scratch.

With the furry suit's arms hanging from his waist, they could see that Parry's entire upper body was covered in long, snaking scars. They spiralled around his slim torso from the groin up to the nape of the neck, and down his arms, purposeful in appearance and agonisingly methodical. In places they were as much as a quarter of an inch deep, vividly pink but completely and cleanly healed.

Priscilla stared, tracing her eyes slowly along the grooves on Parry's body like a needle across a record. Parry felt a cool, exploratory touch on his shoulder and turned.

Doggo pulled his hand back quickly, with the look of a man who has woken from a sleepwalk to find himself embracing a lit three bar fire.

'I recognise these...' he said. 'I recognise these. The woman I told you about. She had scars, and it was as if I recognised them.'

'Where did you get them from?' said Priscilla, almost as if she was speaking to herself.

Parry ran his fingertips gently along the neat new furrows in his skin.

'I don't know,' he said, 'I suppose they gave them to me.'

'Ruthie had scars,' said Doggo.

Parry's fingers followed the spiralling grooves across his ribs and around to the back as far as he could go.

'Were they like this?' he said.

'No. But it was like I knew them. It was like déja vu, but like...' Doggo's hands made chopping, frustrated movements as he searched for the words.

'Déja vu for things you haven't seen yet,' said Priscilla.

They both looked at her.

'*What?*' she said.

'No. No. That's right,' said Parry.

Doggo rubbed at the back of his neck.

'What do we do now?' he said.

'Why do we have to do anything?' said Priscilla, as she began to slide on the sides of her feet back down the slope towards the water.

'We have to see Charles Bigger,' said Parry. 'He's at the centre of it all. It's him that made it all happen.'

'But we don't have any idea where he is,' said Doggo. 'You know this place is the size of a town. There are thousands of people trapped here, God knows how many of his people. And he could be anywhere—'

Priscilla's voice echoed up from below.

'He's at the Bigger International Hotel.'

'I'm trying to talk to you. Come back up here,' said Parry. 'How do you know that?'

She squatted down on her haunches and made gentle ripples in the water with the tips of her fingers.

'I don't have the slightest idea how I know. I don't even know where I've been. I just know that's where he is.'

Now Parry and Doggo stood at the water's edge together, looking at the back of Priscilla's head. Parry put his hand on her shoulder and she shrugged it away violently as she stood.

'Don't touch me. I'm not going there. I will not go there, do you understand, Parry? I will not go there. Look what they did to you, Parry. Look at yourself. They did something to you, those things have altered your mind. I think they've rubbed out my mind as well. I can't remember a fucking thing anymore. Why would they do a thing like that unless they were trying to hide something? It's just... forget it...'

She seemed to have worn herself out, and she turned away from them fiercely to throw a chip of concrete out across the water. It hopped three times before disappearing, three circles of water radiating out across the smooth surface.

Parry watched her stiff tense back and frightened little hands for a few seconds. Doggo, experienced in knowing when to join in a discussion and when to become furniture, hung back at a discreet distance.

'Priscilla,' Parry said, 'listen. I mean really, how can we ever know that what we think our own decisions really *are* our own decisions?'

She half looked at him over her shoulder.

'Fine. You get as metaphysical as you like, Parry. But I know he's there and I am not going to that hotel with you. No way. I mean what do you think you're going to do? How are things going to better if you go there?'

'That's what I don't know yet. But I have to do something. Perhaps just be there when it all, whatever it is, when it all happens.'

'You've changed, Parry,' she said, and turned away from him again.

Parry looked at Doggo, who had his hands in pockets like he desperately wanted to go somewhere, maybe the toilet.

'Your friend might not be—' Parry began, but didn't know how he could finish the sentence or the day.

'I know,' said Doggo, 'Ruthie's dead. We're alive though, aren't we? We seem to be alive. And the end to it all is up there.'

They shook each other's hand and some primal masculine agreement thing passed silently between them.

'I don't want to leave you here, Pris,' said Parry.

She waved a dismissive hand backwards. 'I'll still be here when you get back.'

Parry stood helplessly behind her, hunched up and ready to explode with words, then let his shoulders fall. He knew there was nothing more he could say. He began to work his arms back into his costume again. The itching of his scars had gone away. Apparently they were satisfied at having been exposed to public view. His new skin was already starting to feel as unconsciously familiar to him as his old one had.

Priscilla being Priscilla, she couldn't help waiting until Parry and Doggo were up to their knees in the freezing water before she pointed out a boat that she could see dragged halfway up onto the concrete beach in the distance.

(eleven)
boy bingo

Two naked boys squirmed forlornly in the marble foyer of the Bigger International Hotel. Occasionally one of them sobbed involuntarily, unable to choke back the sound any longer, and it echoed up to the hotel's topmost gallery as they danced at gun point for Charles Bigger. Sometimes there was laughter too, from the men who poked them with cold steel gun barrels or mockingly drew them close to whisper tender atrocities in their ears.

The laughter was conveyed to Charles down a mile long matt black tunnel of apathy and ennui. He found himself prey to an ever worsening sense of indifference towards his day and night flesh against rubber against metal against flesh jag. They were no closer to finding his grandfather's body. Charles was continually plagued by unpleasant dreams of the old man's crypt, which had begun to force themselves upon him even when he was awake. His previously ballistic member had shrunk to tiny uselessness. For him, and for everybody around him, this was a disaster with substantial fallout. Now he was reduced to wearing someone else's pyjamas—because he had soiled all of his own and in the last few days had refused to wear anything else—and watching two teenage boys being made to frug and twist feebly as if they were at the fag end of a Californian beach party. Later, some of the men were planning to play Boy Bingo; a combination of an unbridled Caligula-themed orgy and the staid game of chance favoured by old ladies in crimplene at the seaside.

From outside the foyer's glass doors came sporadic bangs, as some men fired their guns into the Family Plaza pool in a bored attempt to torpedo the fish.

Yesterday Charles had been drunk on domination, delirious and out of control. Now he had to deal with the inevitable grisly hangover, and the only thing that could act as the glass of Alka-Seltzer he badly needed was to find Old Man Bigger and make some kind of peace. Kill the thing that chased and snapped at his every thought like a badly trained urban Rottweiler taken to the countryside and let off of the leash.

He reeled one of the reluctant boys towards him by a thin arm. The other lad continued his dance, but his movements became even more spastic and erratically uncertain than before. He had one eye on the casually dangling guns and the other on Charles, undecided which of the two was more life threatening. He didn't understand most of what the men were saying and he was glad of it. The night had been the longest one he had ever known in his short life, and now he wanted it to end. Please, somehow, just end.

'You're shaking,' Charles said, and bit the boy hard on the cheek.

Three floors below them, the Laundry was bereft of purpose. Everything in there smelled of fabric conditioner and damp, slept-in sheets. A row of twenty washing machines stood against the longest wall; their circular doors hung open, freezeframed halfway through a mechanical Busby Berkeley routine. Their dance partners, white plastic rectangular bins on wheels, stood in a ragged chorus line opposite. The machines' open doors looked gaping and hungry for the sheets and towels in the bins that they could never have. They were trapped in a circle of Hell reserved for frustrated domestic appliances.

Parry and Doggo stood in front of the service lift's silver doors, not sure whether or not they dared to press the button which would summon it from above.

'What are we going to do when we meet him?' said Doggo.

Parry stared at the vertical line where the first part of the door concertinaed into the second. 'I don't know,' he said. That simple, just a plain statement of fact.

Doggo nodded his head twice.

'Just checking.'

Parry poked his finger at the button. A white, upward pointing triangle illuminated itself with a tiny click.

As the lift travelled up towards the ground floor of the hotel, Doggo had an impulse to kiss Parry on the cheek. Parry didn't know if it was apprehension and fear that made his pulse quicken and his chest tighten. He asked Doggo why he'd done that; Doggo said that he just felt it was needed at that moment, and he was right. He said he knew that there were lots of possibilities now. Everything was holding its breath and waiting to collapse into one version of events or the other. Two fluorescent strips above them buzzed and the lift purred efficiently upwards.

Doggo and Parry rose. Priscilla had already fled deeper into the ground.

When she heard men's echoing voices and heavy feet splashing through water, and saw the circles of torch beams playing up and down the curved wall, she knew immediately that it wasn't her they were looking for, but also that they wouldn't take too kindly to her presence. With difficulty she ground the bulky metal door along its tracks and locked it into place. She tried to control her panic and move quickly and carefully down the spiral staircase, remembering her fire drill and repeating it like a mantra—proceed in an orderly manner to the nearest designated exit/proceed in an orderly manner to the nearest designated exit—but eventually she had to settle for a controlled slide, scraping her ankles and bruising her buttocks twenty or thirty times over but without the time to feel a thing.

She had forgotten that the crypt had another door.

She hid herself behind a refrigeration unit the size of a telephone box and listened. Over the buzz of the heat dissipating coils she rested her head against, it was difficult to guess how many of them there were, because they were hidden from view by the mass of machinery in the centre of the crypt. Their low chatter and the click of their footsteps reverberated between the vaulted ceiling and bare walls; the acoustics of the room could just as easily have magnified their numbers or deadened the sound of others lurking nearby. At least one of the men was loudly and colourfully expressing annoyance because he couldn't get his radio to work properly. Priscilla crept along the damp wall.

A man wearing a flak jacket and poking at the side of his head, presumably the owner of the annoyed voice, appeared around the side of the cryonic capsule. He stopped in mid step and looked right at the motionless Priscilla, who willed him not to see her. It almost worked. His gaze travelled on past her and then rapidly back again, in a classic doubletake that would have done one of Charlie Bigger's cartoons proud.

'Hey! You!' he shouted and pointed with his free hand, not taking his other hand away from his ear. She realised that he had been tapping his head because he was wearing a hands-free radio.

She had little doubt that he was referring to her. More armed and armoured men appeared from behind the machinery. Priscilla put her hands up, which felt stupid and rather futile, so she put them down again.

The caged bulbs flickered along the bunker's grey walls in sequence, grim industrial fairy lights to mark the celebration of a strange birth.

And in the perfect dark between binary flashes of light, something bulldozed the air between her and the men with its crackling UHF presence. Priscilla imagined that it must feel like this to swim with a whale, its vast alien presence benign but with the undeniable and ever present capacity to drag her under and crush her puny body for trespassing into its element. It existed on a different scale and moved along a different path than she did. The temperature of the already cool air in the room had plummeted by about twenty degrees, and she caught glimpses of her own breath condensing in the air in front of her.

She could see the men silently falling to their knees with fists crammed into eye sockets, or convulsed and stiff and staring at nothing. She saw strobe lit gasping men reaching desperately beneath bullet proof vests to itch at the parasitic truths which had inveigled themselves there. Flash cuts of muscles standing out like suspension bridge cables on taut spasmed necks and drowners' hands reaching out to babyclutch at nothing. They breathed hard and cried out helplessly, sub language, like dreamers in the night. The atmosphere had congealed into a solid block of electricity. Priscilla sank back against the wall, would have pressed herself into its cement if she could have, and closed her eyes tighter than she ever had before, tried to hide herself and hoped that the pure info monster would know that she was not its enemy and pass her over. She was helpless, unable to breathe or out manoeuvre the thing which hummed all around her.

The next thing she saw was a man crawling around in slow circles like someone looking for a dropped contact lens. He seemed to be blind, and quietly pleaded for his mummy to take him home. The others sat hunched and catatonic in the corners they had found and crawled into, or lay in inert, broken toy positions with thousand yard stares and guns or flickering short circuiting torches held loosely in insensate hands. The man with the radio was stretched out face up with his eyes open, headset askew and the mic dangling between his eyes like an angler fish's lure.

There was a sudden deafening bang. Priscilla froze, afraid that she had been shot. When the echoes had died away and she drew breath again, she knew that she hadn't. She inched her head around the side of the silver cylinder. One of Bigger's men had remained conscious enough to blow the back of his own head off next to the orange door. The brain whose every neuron had truly experienced what it was to mean absolutely nothing, had destroyed itself. The splash of matter on the painted door looked more like someone had thrown a jar of strawberry jam against it than blood and brain.

Priscilla stared at the suicide and knew that something had changed in her own head. She turned her attention to the silver pod. How could a stiff in a tin can cause so much trouble? She decided she would get the old man upstairs and hand him over even if she had to drag his rank carcass there in carrier bags.

Above her head, one by one the screws on the canister's lid began to slowly pirouette upwards and fall with minute metallic ticks as they unfastened themselves from the inside.

It was amazingly easy to meet Charles Bigger. Parry and Doggo watched him from behind the coconut palms as he tangoed with the flaccid, unconscious body of a teenage boy. After ten anxious minutes Parry just parted the foliage and strode across the floor as if he owned the place. He tapped Charles on the shoulder. He turned a baleful eye and a heavy calibre handgun on Parry, and Parry wondered where the hell he had been keeping it. The boy was slung under Charles's other arm like a sack of potatoes. Doggo had not been far behind Parry. A quick glance back established that Doggo was now flanked by two of Bigger's men, who had left off tormenting the other boy to poke guns at his head. Doggo had his hands up, which completely failed to make him look harmless.

'Who the hell are you?' said Charles.

'My name's Parry.'

'Parry. Give me one good reason why I shouldn't blow your fucking face off for coming in here and scaring me.'

Parry's hands went looking for pockets that he didn't have. 'Because I know what you're looking for. I know where Charlie Bigger is. I've seen the... cryonic... thing.'

(What a great time to forget how to speak, Parry.)

'Get the fuck away from me... you fuck,' Charles said, a hoarse whisper in a big room.

'I know you've seen him. He comes to you doesn't he? You see things. You see him. You're scared he'll come and take it all away.'

Charles did nothing except begin to lose a staring match with Parry.

'Underneath everything. A silver can with him inside. I've seen what you did. I've seen everything you've done, everything you've ever done in the past is part of my head now and I can't ever forget.'

Bigger's men stood at the far end of the foyer like furniture. Parry took a step forward and he could see a tiny nick a third of the way up the barrel of the gun.

'This is the end,' he said.

'You can't hurt me,' whispered Charles, 'I'm the king of the whole fucking world.'

'You don't understand. That's what I came here for, just to give you a message.'

Charles lowered the gun infinitesimally and blinked his lids down slowly across watery blue bloodshot eyes.

'There's nothing for you in the future. You belong to the past,' Parry said, the words flowing out of him like molten silver now, 'because after today you don't exist.'

The boy sniffed a nosebleed bubble back up his nostril.

Doggo cocked his head slightly as if listening carefully, his hands on the way down from surrender.

Parry became aware of a rattling sound, like somebody driving a tractor on a road. No, not a tractor.

Tank.

It hesitated for a moment, as if conscious and planning its next move, before lurching forwards and bursting explosively through the huge sheet of plate glass at the front of the hotel. The men closest to it put their hands uselessly across their faces as they were pelted with massive chunks of glass which had been yanked from the frame and now broke with skull shattering force across their heads.

Charles dropped his dancing partner on his face and ran. Parry picked the boy up under the arms and did his best to get out of the tank's way with the semi-conscious boy in tow. Doggo had got himself lost in the confusion of falling glass and flying house plants.

The black tank ground its way inexorably over broken glass and uprooted trees to park itself wonkily in the hotel foyer, a bizarrely out of scale interloper amongst the coordinated sofas and coffee tables.

The hatch at the top of the tank swung open and rested heavily on its hinges. Priscilla emerged out of the hole, gesticulating wildly and waving a gun Parry knew she had no idea how to use.

'Parry! It's coming! It's coming!' she said.

One of Bigger's men turned, a cornered and rabid dog, to take aim at the tank. Parry saw it all, but was weighed down by the boy and rooted to the spot as firmly as the broken palms under the tank's tracks for those few seconds that it always takes for a catastrophe to happen.

The first bullet ricocheted off of the tank's armour with a high pitched twang.

The second hit the open hatch door with a dull metallic clunk.

The third hit Priscilla in the stomach. She let out an animal combination of squeal and gasp as all the air was forced out of her lungs and she was thrown backwards like a doll by the bullet's force. She disappeared inside the tank as she fell and Parry couldn't stop himself screaming out at the shocking sight of it.

Charles made it to the swimming pool before the overhead lights began to flicker and spark. The fluorescent tubes could not take any more, and imploded to shower powdered glass into the water. Charles stood still by the edge of the pool and listened to the gentle lapping of the water. Everything in the room was lit from beneath in turquoise by the pool lights. The curve of white plastic poolside chairs. The ubiquitous tropical plants casting long spidery shadows onto the ceiling. A wall of glass bricks picking up the light and refracting it onto a row of exercise bikes, making them into pointillistic cerulean abstracts. And an old man, legendary body, his naked oversized skin hanging flaccidly off of his coat-hanger bones. Grandfather, set free from his nitrogen flask and not in the best of moods.

Charles Bigger, a man manifestly guilty of butchering human beings like pigs in a slaughterhouse and of the most exploitative perversions, wept like a baby. The pistol dropped out of his hand and sank to the bottom of the pool.

The old man's flesh was slightly translucent, pale and amphibian like something blind from a cave. He walked towards Charles with a series of loose jointed motions. His movements didn't bear much resemblance to anything human; they were most akin to a plucked and gutted chicken being operated like a puppet by a fist shoved up its arse.

The old man took Charles's head in his clammy weak hands, and Charles could see the thing's eyes, milky and unfocused with death. As a rough tongue worked its way inside his mouth it tasted powdery and medicinal. Now the vile shrivelled hands were under Charles's pyjamas, obscenely intimate with his every secret place. Old Man Bigger clasped his lisping lizard liar descendent to his rack of ribs like a long lost lover. Grey lips formed words against his face YOU CAME, it said, YOU CAME as Charles breathed to a pulsebeat of voodoo drums, one in each ear. Each inhalation became more difficult than the last, and he began to feel light headed as his lungs were only fractionally filled by his asthmatic gasps. He realised that his grandfather's loving embrace was the past and could not be escaped and that the old man's hands were thin and scratchy but strong and the thing's arms were holding him tight tight tight tighter and now his ribs were starting to give under the industrial pressure and he had the microscopic and momentary consolation of feeling that he had, for the last time in his life, been betrayed. The Charlie Thing's face hung loose, the head thrown back; a dead weight on that emaciated turkey neck. Monster, Charles thought, you monster, and he wasn't sure which of the two Charles Biggers was thinking it. He felt his organs begin to haemorrhage and burst inside him. Thoughts exploded randomly across the viewfinder of his brain. The Charlie Thing let Charles fall and he died on the way to horizontal. As he expired he thought about all the different coloured and intertwined routes on a London Underground map and wondered why and he went into the blue.

part three

future hug

Nobody was ever entirely sure what happened to Charles Bigger in the end. It was Doggo who found him blanched and dead, his eyes forever open wide, floating face up in the swimming pool wearing his pyjama trousers. An old man's naked prolapsed corpse lay at the edge of the pool, slowly leaking a watery brownish fluid into the deep end.

The sound of an angry gang of marauding tourists came from the foyer as they scrambled through the smashed plate glass windows. Armed with golf clubs and queuing posts, their Palaeolithic hunting instincts had surged to the fore. They cornered and crippled their erstwhile tormentors as efficiently and ferociously as a Siberian tribe bringing down a woolly mammoth. Putters and six irons rose and fell, smashing knees and shattering ankles. The gun men, bereft of purpose and drained of malice, surrendered by default. They let out wretched screams as they were beaten, their voices high and girlish, but the tourists did not want them to die. Parry and Doggo left Bigger to shrivel in the water and quietly withdrew.

The summer-cold night came to an end. The Amusement World had a raw and primordial splendour as they watched the sun rise over it from the roof of the Bigger International. An entire quadrant of the park—from the Enchanted Chateau to the largest Fast Foods of the World Restaurant cluster—was either burning, or already blackened and desolated. The skeletons of buildings and rides reached into the air in warped, ruined arcs. Tourists moved in slow dazed packs over the smoking wreckage or ran wildly through the streets, looting gift shops and stealing empty cash registers if they still had the energy. A virtually imperceptible breeze skewed the inky columns of smoke diagonally across the park so that they cast long linear shadows. They striped the Amusement World in two colours, lead and Lucozade.

In the extreme distance, some of the bewildered survivors of the extended package holiday in Hell could just about be seen as microscopic specks shuffling towards the numbered car parks which encircled the Amusement World like a vast frozen moat.

Nearer to them, a group of pubescent girls danced about randomly on the side of a floodlit hill. Their lissome moving bodies cast huge and intricate humanoid shadows on the whitewashed wall of the driving range.

'It's beautiful,' said Parry. 'How can it be beautiful? People died. So many people have died. How can things be so... malicious?'

He realised the futility of words, and gave up on them. Doggo shrugged, then turned back to look towards the golf course again, hidden behind a stand of trees whose upper branches had been wilted by a burning slick of petrol.

'It's not. It's sick and ugly and terrible. It's being alive at the end of it all that's beautiful,' he said, after a very long pause in which the only sounds were an occasional distant shout from below and the soft crump of collapsing beams and walls, too burnt to stand.

'But why me and you and not her?'

'I'm a capacitor, you're a resistor,' said Parry, 'We were all a part of what's happened somehow. I don't know how.'

'She didn't have to die.'

'I don't know. I really don't. I can't even think about it at the moment. Later.'

'Christ,' said Doggo. 'I didn't even find out her surname.'

Doggo turned away from the golf course, and the

reminders of loss it contained, and held onto Parry hard like he was afraid that he would be blown away by the softly moving air that whispered around them. His body shook from its core, and he might have been crying.

'I hate to interrupt such a beautiful scene,' said a woman's voice behind them.

Priscilla was standing on the platform where the stairs emerged onto the roof, with her arms folded across her stomach. She was wearing somebody else's coat. One of the dancing boys trailed in her wake. He was also wearing a coat which evidently didn't belong to him, a formal jacket that was buttoned but hung loose and hollow over his thin bare chest. The other boy walked stiffly behind them both, a duvet grasped tight around his throat. The left side of his face was beginning to swell up and turn purple around the bite mark, his body physically rejecting Bigger's violation. The boy in the jacket hovered anxiously between Priscilla and his friend, his hands ready to catch either one of them should they keel over.

'You're supposed to be lying down, and so is that kid,' said Parry.

'We got bored.'

'You've been shot.'

'Only a little bit.'

Priscilla unfolded her arms and held out the rectangular black shape of a flak jacket which she had been nursing underneath. She wormed her finger inside a ragged hole where the sniper's bullet was still tightly lodged.

'Men don't understand that sometimes your choice of bra can make all the difference,' she said. 'Particularly if it's made of Teflon. And if the thing had fit properly, I bet I wouldn't have felt it a bit.' She lifted up her shirt to rub tenderly at her bruised abdomen. 'As it is, I just feel like I've been kicked by a very pissed off elephant.'

She limped over and put her arms around them both, and she laughed hard like she had once before in the Enchanted Chateau, throwing her head back and showing all of her teeth. She winced and her smile became a grimace, and then a smile again.

'This must be what they call a group hug,' she said. 'If John could see us now... I mean, this is so Amusement World.' But she didn't want to break away and they all felt warm against each other and comfortably human.

'Priscilla?' said Doggo.

'Hmmm?'

'Where the hell did you learn to drive a tank?'

'I don't even know how to drive a car,' said Priscilla. 'I saw it parked there in the Family Plaza, I got in and it just sort of... came to me.'

She shrugged and smiled as if it was just one of those things, then frisbeed the bullet proof vest off the edge of the roof into the Family Plaza.

They established that the boys' names were Anatoly and Nikolai, but could get very little other information out of them because their English was no more intelligible than their Russian. Doggo surmised that they were the sons of nouveau riche Russian capitalists, and nobody cared to argue with him.

Parry wanted to remember the whole thing precisely as he was seeing it now, experience fully the hard earned joy, laced with broken glass, that he felt at that moment. He sucked it all in with every one of his senses turned up to eleven.

The morning sky which was the colour of a deep seated and persistent bruise finally beginning to heal.

The faint smell of melted plastic and burnt grass in the smoke from the buildings below.

Nikolai and Anatoly, squatting on the gravel and chattering away at each other in Russian as if they were the only two people who existed; they had been living on opposite edges of the galaxy and they had a lot of news to catch up on.

The way Priscilla stood there off balance and lopsided as always, a winter coat fallen halfway down her shoulder.

Doggo in a dirty teeshirt stretched tight across his broad chest, both knees grazed and dirty, the thumb of one gigantic hand pressed tightly into the palm of the other, which he had somehow cut in the course of the carnage downstairs.

Parry felt their closeness behind him as he moved towards the edge of the roof and gently rested his hands on the parapet.

They searched the sky for flying saucers.

Alistair Gentry grew up in a windswept British seaside resort where he spent his time amassing a vast collection of Star Wars toys. His short fiction appears in the collections *Allnighter* and *Fission* (Pulp Faction 1997, 1996). *Their Heads are Anonymous* is his first novel.